A Billionaire For Christmas

An Opposites Attract Insta-love Romance

The Blackwell Brothers
Book 4

Kay Lyons

Kindred Spirits Publishing

Dear Readers,

When I finished writing THE GETAWAY GUY, I knew Rhys had to have his own story even though he wasn't a Blackwell brother. That's why I decided to make him an honorary Blackwell and include his story as part of the series. Rhys was just a special guy who needed his own happily-ever-after. So...here it is.

:)

Happy reading!

A Billionaire For Christmas

Chapter One

Come join us in the Bahamas. Don't spend Christmas alone."

Rhys Lachlan stared out from his penthouse suite on the upper floors of the Lachlan Hotel and Resort in Carolina Cove, North Carolina, and watched as the moon cast a silvery line over the ocean below. "I'll be fine, Mother."

"But you'll be alone."

His lips twisted, but he couched his thoughts and said, "I'm never alone. You know that. And there was an issue here with the contractor at the hotel going up in Southport. I wanted to take care of it in person."

His mother scoffed, and the sound carried over the phone.

"Bodyguards and hotel maids aren't family, darling."

They weren't, but the reality of his life meant he'd spent more time with his employees since he'd left for college and then taken his place in the family business upon graduation, than his now-retired, world-traveling parents.

He'd left the hotel suite dark after he'd entered, preferring the shadowy interior to the brightly lit awareness that he was, indeed, going to be alone for the holidays. His grandfather planned to fly down and join his parents for Christmas before flying back home to New York, but Rhys was needed here for the duration.

Obtaining female company was an easy fix should he decide to pursue it, but the women so readily drawn to his money held no appeal. "I'll consider it, but I'm sure Father will appreciate having you all to himself for once." His family had friends the world over, friends who very much wanted to catch up after years and years of living too-busy lives. Like him, his parents were rarely alone.

"You'd really rather stay there?"

The party life of the Bahamas had fired his blood in his younger years, but ever since his engagement to Quinley Anders—an engagement she'd broken when she'd left him at the altar on their wedding day back in the spring—things hit differently. "I'm needed here until the contractor situation has been handled. Besides, I have a few events to attend."

"*Real* events or are you making excuses?"

He smiled at his mother's obvious doubt. "Real," he said, though whether or not he attended the dinners and galas he'd been invited to remained to be seen. "Consider this good PR for the Lachlan name."

"*You* did nothing to taint the Lachlan name. I'm still amazed you've forgiven Quinley for how she treated you. And I'm sure you could've found someone else to handle the issues there so you didn't have to go back. That place must bring back bad memories."

He closed his eyes at the turn the conversation had taken and pinched the bridge of his nose. "I'm not hung up on Quinley if that's what's worrying you. Mother, I told you the day of the wedding that I'd had some doubts myself. She did the right thing calling it off."

"*She* humiliated us for all the world to see."

"Quinley has profusely apologized since then on numerous occasions. You don't have to be happy about what happened, but please accept the fact

Quinley was right to do what she did and leave it at that. If I can forgive her, so can you. Let's just move forward."

He heard his mother inhale before releasing a slow breath.

"Fine. Your father told me that the restaurant is doing well, though how you wound up *working* with Quinley and her new fiancé will forever remain a mystery to me. I'd think you'd hate the man, all things considered."

Maybe he should. But Elias Blackwell hadn't even met Quinley until she'd jumped into the limousine he'd driven the day of their nonwedding. While Rhys liked to prick the man's jealousy when it came to Quinley just because he found it amusing, it *was* truly over between them.

As to offering Elias a place to house Haven, Rhys promised himself long ago that he'd never miss a promising business opportunity because of an emotional stumbling block. When he'd heard the details of Elias Blackwell's dream restaurant, Rhys knew it was viable, especially for areas like Carolina Cove and Wilmington that drew millions of tourists every year from all over the world.

The restaurant was innovative and unique, and he'd wanted to be a part of it because Haven set the resort apart from the other hotels in the area, which was an ongoing goal. That's why he currently pondered whether or not it was too early to approach Elias about expanding Haven's reach and opening other Haven locations within the hotel chain.

His grandfather and father might have started Lachlan hotels, but it was up to him to continue its legacy. "Like I said, you don't have to understand. Just be glad it's worked out so well. Haven has been a huge success and surpassed all our projections." So much so that he felt he would be slacking as the CEO if he didn't make new locations happen.

"I suppose that is a good thing."

He grinned at her lack of enthusiasm.

"Before I forget, I plan to send a few decorators."

His grin quickly faded. "What? Why?"

"Because if you're going to stay there, you need a tree, as does the rest of the hotel."

"How do you know I don't already have one?"

"Because I *know*. The resort should be lit up inside and out for the holidays, and instead you're there in the dark like the Grinch."

He glanced into the darkened interior of his penthouse and shrugged, not bothering to ask how she knew what she knew. Or point out that Quinley had said much the same thing when she'd decorated Haven's interior a few days ago.

Every hotel in the chain had a scheduled and contracted decorator to handle such things, but somehow he'd missed that detail when it came to this one. More proof that he was off his game. "You don't need to send anyone. I'll have my PA take care of it. There are two weeks remaining before the big day. I'll arrange for the hotel to be made festive, *and* I'll get my own tree."

"Will you, though?"

"I will. If you insist I have one, I'd rather pick my own."

"You always did enjoy playing Paul Bunyan and cutting down a tree when we were in the mountains."

He couldn't deny it. There was something primal about going out and choosing just the right tree and then felling it himself. He loved fresh trees over artificial. But right now?

Normally his favorite holiday season, he felt downright Scrooge-ish in nature these days, mostly because he'd planned on spending this Christmas with his new wife in their new home, one he'd built for them along the Cape Fear River.

But he didn't have a wife, and the house sat

empty and unused. Undecorated too. Time to sell the monstrosity. He wasn't sure why he'd held onto it this long. He made a mental note to get the property listed as soon as possible.

"I'll give you a few days to get the hotel *and* your suite decorated. If you don't make it happen, I'm calling in the professionals myself. And don't think of lying to me. I do have spies there, you know."

He chuckled, well aware that his parents had "spies" in every hotel across the massive chain. They might be retired, but they liked keeping tabs on things to make sure the hotels were kept up to standards and morale remained high. "It'll be done."

"Rhys, you might think you're fooling me, but I know you all too well. You've been different since you and Quinley...parted ways," she said diplomatically. "And while I know you had some doubts, you're still my very romantic son, and...I'm worried about you."

"No need to worry."

"It's a mother's duty. You looked forward to the wedding and being married, starting a family, and I *know* you're grieving that loss even if you feel Quinley wasn't quite the right woman."

The words, the images that flickered through his

mind due to them, left him shifting uncomfortably on the balcony.

"Oh, Rhys, honey…"

"I'm fine."

"You're *not*. You haven't dated since Quinley, and I know you've had plenty of offers."

"Not because I'm still in love with her— I'm not. But she's a hard act to follow, and I'm tired of the dating scene. Of being looked at like a dollar sign. And I get that most men wouldn't care, but…I do."

"Of course you do. But in order to find this new special someone, you have to go *out*."

"Maybe not. Maybe, if I'm patient, she'll… appear. Like a Christmas gift under the tree."

A soft laugh filtered over the phone, but it was tinged with sadness. "Well, for that to happen, we might have to contact Oliver Beck's wife, the matchmaker. What is her name again?"

"Marsali. And I'm *not* ready for a matchmaker, so don't even think about adding that to my Christmas gifts, Mother."

"Fine," she said, laughter audible in her voice. "But you can't stay in and *work* all the time. It wasn't good for your grandfather or your father, and it's certainly not good for you."

"I go out."

"To work functions and networking events. When was the last time you did something for you? Something just for fun? You need to...*find* your Christmas spirit, darling. Especially *this* year of all years. Don't allow what happened last spring to steal that from you."

He hated to admit his mother had a point. "Okay. I'll go out and—find a Christmas tree. How's that?"

"It's a start. But I want to see pictures so I know it's done. I'll be able to tell if your heart is in it."

He sighed, knowing she'd harass him until he followed through. "I'm going to get off here and go grab dinner from upstairs, but I'll call you again soon."

"And you'll think about joining us for Christmas? Your grandfather misses you. We all do. You've been traveling so much since spring. And we can discuss hiring Marsali—when you're ready, of course."

"I'll think about it."

She didn't seem happy with his response but murmured her love before they said goodbye.

Rhys shoved the phone in his pocket on his way through the suite to the door.

Whether subconsciously or not, he *did* mourn

the life he'd hoped to have, and it was time to stop. He'd always loved the holidays, to the point of being that ridiculous person driving everyone insane with holiday cheer, going overboard with presents and trips and all things good in the name of Christmas. His grandmother was to blame, and since he'd spent so much of his childhood staying with her while his grandfather and his parents traveled on hotel business, her love of the holidays had seeped into his blood.

He had a life and lifestyle *any*one would envy. It was time to come up with a plan. And the first step?

Decking the halls.

Chapter Two

Nothing said it was the season like grumpy, indecisive customers and frozen toes.

Sara Zennick stared at the group giving her a headache because every time they chose a tree and she rung them up, they suddenly had second thoughts and found another they liked better. She fought her impatience, trying to maintain a friendly smile while keeping an eye on the others roaming the tree lot.

Her family had supplied Christmas trees to Carolina Cove for generations and was the only tree lot permitted on the island. A long-ago contract made with the powers-that-be guaranteed them the coveted position.

She stared at the couple as the woman wandered

off again, despite saying *this* was the tree she wanted —for the fifth time—and Sara tapped her frozen toes in her too-thin boots. She hadn't had to sell trees since her senior year of high school, so she'd forgotten just how cold the air could be on the island between the Atlantic and the Cape Fear River once the sun set.

The woman's husband gave Sara a shrug and followed dutifully off after his wife. Sara dragged the fifth not-good-enough tree back to its spot and left it, turning in time to see a different couple fast-walking toward an SUV with a tree they hadn't purchased. "Excuse me. Hello? You need to pay for that!"

The couple broke into a run, neither looking back at her as they tossed the tree on top of the vehicle and hurried inside, taking off with a crunch of tires on gravel before she managed to make it around the trees and people to the parking area. "You've got to be kidding me."

The thieves nearly hit a car on the way out of the lot while she fumed and wondered how she'd tell her father. They lost a few trees every year due to them drying out or damage, but outright thievery was usually a middle of the night thing—not right there during regular hours. "The spirit of Christmas is officially dead because of *you*!"

"What happened?" a man asked as he exited an SUV and approached her, a frown on his handsome face.

She continued to glare at the vehicle speeding away, the thieves' arms out the window to hold the tree atop the roof.

It was bad enough she'd lost her job due to an unexpected company layoff, but the stolen tree hit her like a smack in the face, hard and without warning.

With a car payment, student loan debt and her ridiculous rent, she'd been forced to give up her tiny yet beautiful apartment and return home to the tree farm.

The timing helped her parents, though, since her dad refused to be anywhere but at the hospital after her mother's car accident. Still, the blows kept coming. During her time working the lot since Thanksgiving weekend, she'd now had a blatant theft—and spent countless time being made fun of by teenagers because of the costumes her parents *insisted* she wear as part of the Zinnick's Tree Farm buying experience.

Her phone buzzed in her pocket, and she yanked it out to see her father's face. He called every hour or so to check in, but she needed to get back to the desk and the— "No, no, no," she said, running as fast as she could in the constricting costume to the checkout table only to see that nightmares could indeed get worse.

The cash box was gone.

She whirled around, vaguely acknowledging that the man from the SUV and his companion had followed her, and searched for any sign of whomever might've taken the metal box.

Other than a few people wandering idly through the trees or helping themselves to coffee and cocoa, she saw nothing unusual.

They couldn't have gotten away already, could they? She hadn't left it unattended for *that* long.

Words flitted through her mind, none of them PG as she desperately searched for the culprit, fighting back the hot sting of tears.

"What are you looking for?"

She sank onto the chair behind the portable table, unable to hold back a derisive sound. "Someone stole a tree—while someone else took the cashbox."

The man turned to search the crowd as she'd done, as did the other guy near him obviously listening to the conversation.

She ignored them both and buried her face in her black-gloved hands.

The cash box held the card reader, earnings for the day, *and* the spare change, and without it... "We're closing," she called out, her voice hoarse. "I'm sorry, but—unless you have exact cash for payment, I-I'm afraid I can't sell any more trees tonight. I'm sorry."

"Mommy, I wanna tree! You *promised*," a little girl whined loudly.

The hole Sara wanted to dig and hide inside of needed to be *big* with all the guilt she carried right now. Her father had trusted her to do this *one* little thing, and so far, it had been a disaster.

Normally customers used cards to cash at about seventy-thirty, but today had been mostly cash, and they'd had a decent day's sales up until then. Which meant the money wasn't safely tucked away in an account her father could transfer out of, but gone for good.

The crowd quickly dispersed after checking wallets and purses before sliding her pitying looks. She apologized again and watched them go with a knot in her stomach, hearing the little girl's cries because they had to leave without a tree.

They were the only lot on the island, but there

were others not too far away. No doubt they'd just drive over the bridge to one of them and get a tree there to make the little girl happy again.

She needed to call her father. And the police.

"I'll take them," the man closest to her said.

She blinked, the fog crowding her brain pushing away everything until all that remained was what a failure and disappointment she was to herself and to her family in their time of need. One more burden to worry about when they were drowning in others. "I'm sorry, what?"

She finally managed to focus on the man standing nearby, his arms crossed over his chest.

He looked familiar. So familiar.

Short, dark hair fell slightly longer over his forehead, and the string lights crisscrossed around the lot above their heads hinted at the barest of silver at his temples. Piercing, dark eyes focused unwaveringly on her, but she wasn't able to make out the color.

He was tall, around six feet—give or take an inch, she'd guess—and dressed nicely in slacks and a crisp button-down beneath an elegant coat. He didn't look like a local. They tended to dress more casually and not look like a model.

"I said I'll take them. The trees."

She blinked at him. "Oh, of course. You have cash, I guess. Um, which one do you want?"

A slow smile pulled at his full lips, and she found herself watching it happen like it was slow-mo. The fluttery thrill that filled her came out of nowhere, blindsiding her, since men were not on her wish list for the foreseeable future, what with her life such a mess at the moment as an unemployed woman living back home with her parents.

"All of them."

Chapter Three

Sara blinked and then blinked again, sure she'd misheard him. Maybe the stress had finally gotten to her, and she was having a stroke? "I'm sorry, what?"

"I'll take all of them," he said patiently. "That truck is for delivery, yes?"

"Yeah, it is but—" She looked around, but only the two men had stayed behind after her cash-only announcement. "Is this a joke?"

A frown overtook his model-worthy face, and the man stepped toward the table.

"It's not a joke. I can't do anything about what happened with the tree or the cash box, but I can take the rest of the trees off your...raccoon hands."

The second guy made a noise that sounded like a

choked laugh he tried to disguise. She glared at him and then turned it on the jokester himself. "Haha. Seriously, *not* in the mood, dude. I need to call the police and make a report, so if you're done..."

The guy opened his wallet and studied the contents.

"I'll make a deposit to secure the purchase and pay the rest first thing in the morning. Will that work?"

He handed her a stack of hundreds, twenties, and five dollar bills. Not a couple. A freaking *stack*. Sara went back to blinking. "Are these *real*?"

The second guy outright laughed this time, and she shot him her best corporate glare. The layoff had done a number on her self-esteem because she'd been so blindsided by the news after rearranging her life in order to take the position. But she wasn't an idiot.

"They're real, sweetheart."

Her cell buzzed again and again until she finally answered. "Dad, I can't talk right—"

"Sara? Are you okay? I saw what happened on the camera," her father said in his booming voice.

She held the phone away from her ear because he was *that* loud without being on speaker.

"The police are on the way. I already called them."

She'd forgotten all about the motion camera her father kept on the camper behind her. The notifications also pinged her phone, but it had been buried deep inside the folds of the costume and, truthfully, it went off each time anyone ventured too near the table, so that meant it was constantly pinging and she'd quickly started to ignore it. "Dad, I'm *so* sorry. I got distracted when someone took off with a tree, and when I got back to it the cashbox was gone."

"Things happen, honey. It'll be all right."

But it *wouldn't* be. It was yet another blow to her father when he barely kept his head above water now, what with her mother's medical expenses already rolling in from the many surgeries she'd required—with more to come in the months ahead.

The man shifted in front of her, and she focused on the cash in his hand. "Dad? H-how many trees are here again?"

"I'd say about fifty now given the sales tallies. Honey, do you need me to call Buck to come back? Or...tell the city we have to cancel the contract? If it's too much for you—"

"No. Don't you dare. Buck's needed at the farm, and I can handle this," she said, aware that the man across from her listened to every word.

"Buck wouldn't mind. You know how much he likes you."

Mr. Handsome's gaze narrowed at the news.

"Dad, I need to go. I have a customer."

"Your mama's waking up anyhow. Call me after you talk to the police."

"I will," she said softly. "Let me know what the doctor says when he does rounds. I love you. Give Mama a hug for me."

"Love you, darlin'. Don't worry. It'll all work out, but I'll tell Buck—"

Sara ended the call and tucked the phone into her pocket.

"Your mother is in the hospital?"

She nodded and shoved herself to her frozen feet, legs and back aching after a long day and the unfamiliar mattress inside the camper. "Yes," she said, not giving any further information. "You said you want...*all* the trees?"

The man's smile transformed his face, and she had that same niggle of *I know him* hit her once again. But from where? How? "Did you ever work in Raleigh?"

"No, I haven't."

"Oh. Sorry, you just— You look familiar."

"I have one of those faces. Everyone says so."

The man behind him lifted a hand to his mouth. Or was that to cover a smile? Was she missing something here?

Sara hugged her arms around her front in an attempt to stay warm with the sudden adrenaline drop and ridiculous raccoon costume. Who'd ever heard of a Christmas raccoon? "Well, there are about fifty trees here. And I can deliver," she said, unsure of how she'd make it happen, but she would one way or another, "for a price." She pulled an exorbitant amount out of thin air and waited.

The guy didn't balk. If anything, he seemed amused by her attempt to negotiate, but if she had to hire a few guys to load and unload trees at two locations, she had to cover the cost.

"Sounds fair. I'll take them all and let you know if I need more."

"More?"

"I have a few big projects to do. Keep that as a deposit, and I'll return in the morning with the remainder."

"Um, okay," she said, grabbing a pen. "The delivery address?"

The man rattled off a street address as the police arrived. Sara quickly counted the money and noted it on the pad before tucking it safely away.

She then handed the man a hastily scribbled receipt.

That done, Sara sighed and braced herself to have to admit her stupidity in leaving the cashbox behind to chase after the tree-stealing couple.

The two men moved away, but she noted they didn't leave the area. Instead they helped themselves to the coffee she'd brewed before everything had gone wrong.

Normally her parents would be there dressed in costumes like the one she wore. Her mother had amassed quite a collection over the years and made it part of the tree-buying experience along with coffee and cocoa.

Sara had taken on the job alone, confident it couldn't be *that* hard if her aging parents could handle it. After all she'd navigated corporate board-rooms and the messy bar scenes where the majority of business negotiations had taken place. Selling Christmas trees to tourists and locals? She'd done it as a teenager—with her parents—but she was an adult now. *Pfftt.* Easy, right?

"You had a robbery?"

Yeah, not so easy at all.

Chapter Four

That's a lot of trees, boss," Axel said as they sipped the surprisingly good coffee provided.

There was a sign listing the prices for drinks on the table, and Rhys dipped into his wallet again only to remember he'd given his cash to the beautiful *raccoon.*

"I got it, boss," Axel said, stuffing some bills into the box before picking up his coffee again.

Rhys smirked at the curiosity evident in Axel's tone, amused that he could still manage to surprise his bodyguard on occasion. "Earlier today, my mother pointed out that the entire resort should be decorated for the holidays by now. They won't be wasted."

"I've heard people donate real trees afterwards, to help with the dunes and erosion," Axel offered.

Rhys tucked that bit of information into the back of his mind and made a mental note to have his PA look into it, since it would make for easy disposal while aiding the environment.

The woman—Sara—talked to the police and gave them what information she could. He blatantly eavesdropped, picking up whatever bits she revealed, all the while watching her in her ridiculous costume. Parents' tree lot, *eighty* years of service to the island, father with mother at a hospital after a bad car accident. Mostly cash in the box that had been stolen.

A low sound left Rhys at her story, and drew her attention to him momentarily. Even in the dim light of the many bulbs draped throughout the lot, he was able to make out the flush rising into her cheeks now that she'd removed her mask to speak to the police.

The officers left cards with contact information, and Sara offered them a free cup of hot coffee for the road. The two accepted it gratefully and approached the table.

Rhys dipped his head in greeting before sidling away, hoping they didn't recognize him and call him out. He liked the fact Sara wasn't able to identify him just yet.

"Sorry about that," she said. "Did you need something else?"

Rhys took a look around and frowned. Carolina Cove was packed with people spending Christmas and New Years at the coast, but it was getting late, and this stretch of the island—while perfect for a pop-up tree lot—was isolated. He glanced at the tiny camper painted bright Christmas red and frowned. "Is that where you sleep?"

He didn't like the thought of that. Not at all.

"Glamping all the way," she said in a wry tone that fell short of a sarcastic version of the holiday song. "It's the only way to keep an eye on inventory. Not that that's worked out so well for me today."

He frowned at her before sending a glance toward Axel and back again. "You should go home tonight. If the trees get stolen, I'll take the hit."

Her eyes widened a bit. "Uh, no, it's fine."

"You don't live nearby? You mentioned Raleigh. Is that where you live?"

She had a smattering of freckles across her nose and cheeks, inky dark hair, and ridiculously bright green eyes that drew him like a siren to the depths of the sea. Rhys couldn't remember the last time he'd been so drawn to someone—especially someone dressed as a raccoon.

"I used to but— You know, don't worry about me. I'm fine here. And unfortunately we lose a few trees every year to theft. First time for the cashbox, though."

He frowned at the camper. "I assume it locks from the inside? Do you have some form of personal protection?"

Without being asked, Axel moved behind the table to the camper and opened the door.

"Hey!"

Rhys and Sara watched as Axel took in the lock with a frowning look. "Not much of one. But it does lock," the man grumbled with a shake of his head.

"Yeah, it does, and that's none of your business." Sara stomped over and slammed the camper door shut, raccoon tail swishing behind her as she glared up at the bodyguard. "Who are you again?"

Answering that question might lead to others, so Rhys waved a hand in a silent order for Axel to back off. Sara watched them both warily and Rhys lifted his hands, palms out in front of him, and flashed her a smile. "Apologies. It's just after what happened, you can't blame us for being concerned about your safety."

"I can when I don't even know you," she shot back.

"There are gentlemen still left in the world." He might not always claim to be one, but he'd always protect a woman's safety.

"Look, I have stuff I need to do to close up, so if you don't mind... It's been a day."

Leave, yeah, he got it. Dipping his head in acknowledgment, he took a step back. "I'll return tomorrow morning with the rest of the payment. Stay safe, Sara."

He felt Sara's gaze boring a hole into his back as Axel followed him toward the parking area. Once they were out of earshot, he glanced at Axel. "Would it be weird to have someone watch over her tonight?"

"Given the theft, I'd say it's reasonable. Though I can't say that you've ever asked anyone to watch over a raccoon."

He chuckled. "Maybe Quinley was right, and I am a creeper." His ex had hated her personal security detail and the reports they'd give him at the end of the day. It truly wasn't a matter of him invading her privacy as much as it was protecting her from the danger that came from being associated with him. Kidnapping and ransom, not to mention death threats, had to be considered when someone had as much money as his family.

He'd only ever placed protection on his loved

ones, exes included, but knowing Sara was alone in that little camper…

Axel's grin flashed in the darkness around them.

"Only when it comes to ladies of interest, sir."

Rhys chuckled and resigned himself to the news he was a borderline stalker but then shrugged. "She shouldn't be here by herself, and it sounds as though her family is in trouble. Call one of the guys. Make sure he keeps watch." He admired the fact that Sara tried to help her family in their time of need. Not all families had that kind of relationship. It also didn't hurt that while she was wearing a raccoon costume, he still found her intriguing.

"Consider it done, sir."

Chapter Five

The following morning, Sara glared at the elf costume and groaned.

She yanked the thick candy cane tights on and then grumbled her way into the green shirt and poofy red crinoline skirt, a black stretchy belt cinching everything into place like a Santa belt.

Elf ears and a festive hat her mother had hand-made to match completed the ensemble. Now all she needed was the pointy-toed shoe toppers, and she could call herself a Christmas elf.

A glance in the mirror once she finished dressing left her frowning. She *liked* the costumes with masks because they gave her some anonymity and helped with the embarrassment she felt at wearing them. She understood that some people were a little

Christmas-crazy—her mother especially—but maybe she could find something else? Something a little more...understated?

Her mind scoffed as she glanced at the colorful closet of costumes. The odds were not in her favor there...

Glaring at the mirror, she added a final dusting of glitter face powder to her cheeks and nose and called it good enough.

Her mother demanded to see picture proof every day that she was actually wearing the costumes, claiming it made her smile, so Sara forced a grin for her phone and snapped, sending the photo off to her bedridden mom before stomping toward the camper door.

She liked weekdays on the lot because it was closed until four, and that left her mornings and days mostly free. But weekends meant being open by ten and all day long, making for a ten-hour day.

She unlocked the lock she now considered questionable—thanks for *that*, big scary dude—and stepped out to find a man parked right outside the lot, leaning against his car with a cup of coffee and phone in hand.

When he heard her emerge, he said hello and toasted her with a lift of his cup, but he stayed where he was and continued scrolling as though waiting for someone.

She'd dumped her purse out before showering this morning, and now wore the crossbody as a cash box with half of the five hundred dollar deposit tucked safely inside for change. If the customer from last night actually showed up this morning as planned, she'd make a quick deposit just to be safe.

Sara turned to get the supplies for the beverage table ready to go for the day when the SUV from last night rolled onto the lot and parked beside the waiting man.

She growled out her frustration that she hadn't been mindful enough after tossing and turning most of the night thinking of dark eyes and a handsome face to remember today might not be a normal day. If he took the trees, she wouldn't have any to sell— which meant she didn't need to wear a costume.

But it made Mama happy. So there was that, at least.

She'd texted her father once she'd settled in for the night but hadn't mentioned the late-day tree sales because she hadn't wanted to get his hopes up. What if the man didn't return? Or changed his mind and wanted the equivalent five trees he'd paid for but no more?

The two men from last night exited the Mercedes, and she barely stifled her groan as the tree buyer's gaze raked over her as though memorizing every detail before his face broke with a heart-stopping smile.

But even more surprising was the fact the driver of the SUV paused to talk to the man standing at his car.

Did they know each other? Or were they just making casual conversation?

"Good morning," her customer said, leaving his friend behind to join her. "You're looking awfully grumpy for a Christmas elf."

She lifted her chin and decided to *own* her ridiculous costume because—what else could she do? It made her mama happy, and right now every smile counted when she was in so much pain. "I haven't had my coffee yet," she said. "You came back."

"I said I would."

"Yes, I suppose you did," she murmured. "Still planning on buying them all?"

"I am. Is that a problem?"

Buck would bring a load to replenish the lot either way, so— "Not at all. Can I ask what you're going to do with so many trees?"

His handsome face broke into a smile once again,

one that reminded her of the *details* of the dreams she'd had of him last night. A hot rush flooded her bloodstream.

"Decorate them," he said simply.

"All of them?"

"Every single one," he drawled in a knee-weakening voice. "Would you like to help me, Sara? It might help you regain some of that Christmas spirit you say is dead."

She blinked and frowned. "When did I say that?"

"Yesterday, when you yelled it at the tree thieves."

"Oh, yeah, I guess I did."

He held out a thick envelope, and their fingers brushed when she took it from him.

"So is that a yes? You'll help me with the trees? I wouldn't mind the company."

Yeah, she doubted he lacked company in any way. "My Christmas spirit is in the negative numbers this year, so—I'll pass. But thanks for this," she said, waving the envelope.

He'd paid five hundred down as a deposit last night but fifty trees averaging a hundred dollars each added up, and he hadn't even asked for a bulk discount or argued her delivery fee.

She quickly counted the money despite the little sticky bank strips holding them bunched in thousand-dollar increments. It was her parents' money and not her own, so she had to be sure it was accurate—and real. So she marked the bills with the extra counterfeit marker she'd found inside the camper since the other one had been inside the stolen cash box. And like the bills he'd given her last night, they all passed the test.

The man—men, because his friend had joined them and now stood nearby while the other one had climbed back into his car and remained waiting—watched her with curious expressions as she checked the bills. Finally she finished. "I'll, um, need time to load and deliver the trees, but I'll try to have them to the address you gave me sometime today."

She'd forgotten to look up the address last night because she'd been so out of sorts, but it was on the island, so it wasn't a matter of travel time so much as loading and unloading time, and the man--or woman —power to do it. Hopefully she could scrounge up some hourly help with a quick Facebook post.

"I've got that covered."

She blinked up at him. "What?"

"After I left, I considered the fact you were here alone last night and how you might be again today, so

I brought help. Assuming we're able to use the truck?"

She followed the lift of his chin to where the old red flatbed truck sat with Zinnick Tree Farm emblazoned on the doors in green and gold. "But you paid for delivery."

"If we use the truck, you're still delivering the trees," he said easily.

A van pulled onto the lot, the doors marked with a logo she couldn't make out from where they were by the camper.

He turned toward the four young men climbing out of the van, all dressed in matching work shirts and pants, and waved a hand toward the trees. "Load all the trees onto the truck, guys. Thanks."

A series of "yessir" followed as the men immediately went to work, one climbing onto the bed as the other three began carrying trees for him to stack.

While they did that, the man in front of her shoved his hands into the pockets of his jeans and ambled closer to her.

"Once they're finished loading, I'll ride with you to deliver them."

"I'm sure you'd be much more comfortable in your Mercedes." And the last thing she needed was tall, dark and distracting sitting beside her, watching her fumble the old manual truck from one gear to another. She hadn't had a lot of practice in recent years, though she'd driven it thousands of times.

"I insist. I can help you navigate to the proper areas for unloading."

It wasn't an unreasonable request. Or offer. Especially from someone who'd cleared out the lot. "Fine. I suppose that'll be okay. I'll... I'll go change."

"No, leave it on. I like it. You look adorable, and someone will be there to snap a few photos to mark the occasion."

She glanced at the rapidly emptying lot as more trees continued to be stacked on the truck by the men. They were making record time. "I suppose it wouldn't hurt," she said, reminding herself that her parents deserved all the help they could get. If it cost her a little humiliation, so be it. It was nothing compared to the pain and humiliation her mother endured while nurses and doctors helped her live at the moment. "Thank you again for the business. My — My parents will be thrilled."

"You're very welcome. Now about your lack of holiday spirit..."

She held up her hands and shook her head. "I'm good. You can take my share this year."

"That's not acceptable. Besides, I like a challenge."

"I'm not a challenge," she said. "I mean, not that I'm *easy*. I just meant—"

His chuckle warmed her from head to toe and all the places in between.

The warmth in his dark gaze quickened the normally steady thrum of her heart, and she fought to regain her composure. Any other time, she'd be all for meeting a gorgeous man, but now? Jobless, homeless, and with her life so up in the air? Her mom needing her help the moment she was released from the hospital? This wasn't a good time. The last thing she *needed* was a man. "Let's just...get the trees to wherever they're going so we can both be about our days, shall we?"

Chapter Six

Rhys couldn't stop his smile due to Sara's prim and decidedly pointed response. He wondered if there was a porcupine costume in the camper because it might better fit her prickly attitude at the moment.

A longer look at the delicate shadows beneath her eyes that the glittery makeup couldn't conceal reminded him that she had a lot going on.

"All loaded, sir," one of the men called.

"We'll meet you there," he said. "I'm riding with Ms. Zinnick."

She looked grumbly but excused herself to retrieve the keys to the truck along with her ID. He watched as she locked up the camper and then followed her to where the truck sat waiting.

The puffy crinoline skirt rode up her candy-cane-striped thighs as she climbed in, and he enjoyed a long look before moving round to get in beside her.

She looked absolutely adorable in her costume, facing a wheel twice her width as she got them off to a chugging start. The old truck purred like a champ as Sara rolled them off the lot, onto the roadway. She shifted gears with the grace of a ballerina. "I don't know a single woman—other than you—that can drive a stick shift. I'm thoroughly impressed."

She glanced at him as they bounced along, a pleased flush to her sparkly cheeks.

"I learned to drive it before my legs were long enough to reach the pedals. My dad sat me on his lap and we drove around the farm. He did the pedals, and I was in charge of the steering and gears."

He smiled at the image, that aspect of her life, because of the love reflected on her expressive face. "I bet you had a fun childhood."

"The best," she said softly. "Though I never knew how lucky I was until I went to college. I mean, obviously everyone has a story, but it wasn't until then that I realized how...*good* my story was. That's why one day, I'd love to share it by—"

She broke off abruptly and shook her head, the

act firing every brain cell inside him to know her secret. "You'd like to share it by...what?"

She gave him another furtive glance. "I suppose it wouldn't hurt to tell you since I won't see you again."

He frowned at that, not liking that thought at all.

"I've always dreamed of writing children's books," she said softly, like she truly shared a secret. "About living on the farm and the animals and the Christmas trees. It's...what I've been working on in the camper before I open on weekdays, to keep busy."

And from worrying about her mother no doubt. "Those sound like amazing stories. I'd love to read them sometime."

She flashed him another glance as though assessing whether or not he meant it and seemed to deem him sincere.

"Having to wear these crazy costumes has brought back so many memories of my mom wearing them when I was growing up. I'm writing down ideas as fast as I can between shifts. It's probably silly and nothing will ever come of it. I mean, doesn't *every*one want to write a book these days?"

"That doesn't sound silly at all. Will you illustrate your stories as well?"

She focused on the road as a car passed them and nodded. "Yeah, but for now it's just a dream. Maybe one day."

He heard the wistfulness in her tone. "Dreams can become reality. You just have to pursue them. Tell me more about your mom. What's she like? You said she was in an accident?"

She nodded as they bounced along the road. "My mom is *energy* in human form. She never stops moving. I'd...just left Raleigh and moved back home when my dad called about the accident. Some idiot texting and driving while flying down the road. Mom *died* on the surgical table during the first operation."

Shock and pain radiated off her at the words. "I'm so sorry, Sara. But she's doing better now?"

Her grip tightened on the wheel, and she swallowed audibly. This wasn't exactly Christmas-spirit-inducing conversation, but he wanted to know more about her. Wanted to know everything. And while he could get the details from an investigator's report, he'd much rather hear it from the source.

"Yeah, but she's been in ICU all this time. They only just moved her to a regular room. When Dad mentioned the tree lot and having to break the contract to stay with her, I heard his heart breaking all over again. So I volunteered to cover the lot because it was the only thing I knew I could do to help since I couldn't even get in to see her at the time. It means so much to them, to *both* of them, to keep the contract. And then I lost the cashbox."

He watched her shake her head and frowned. "You didn't lose it, sweetheart. It was stolen. Big difference there, and it could've happened to anyone, especially when they're as worried and distracted as you are about your parents. Turn right up here and keep going straight."

She slowed the truck and made the turn, handling the gears like a pro as she pointed the truck toward the Atlantic.

"Thanks for saying that."

"I meant it. Things happen, and we have to roll with the punches."

"I suppose. We're running out of houses. Which one is yours?"

"Just keep going straight."

"Straight leads right to that hotel."

"It does. Pull up to the side there," he said, pointing to the left.

Sara sucked in a sharp breath and jerked her head toward him, her gaze wide as she looked at him. "Something wrong?"

"You're Rhys Lachlan."

Chapter Seven

Rhys saw the change in Sara's expression, in her body, when she put two and two together. Only it wasn't the reaction he'd expected.

People tended to change around him in ways that set him on edge. Fake politeness, greedy smiles. Whatever it took to be a friend who'd get the benefits of his family's wealth in one way or another.

And the women... Women turned flirtatious, coy —even predatory. But Sara?

She turned distant, like a wall went up right in front of his eyes. The warmth and light in her expression faded, and her eyes took on a wary coolness. "I am. Is that a problem?"

She made the final turn and rolled the rumbling

truck to a halt, drawing the attention of everyone on the street.

"No, not at all. It's just not every day a billionaire wants to slum it in a Christmas tree truck."

His gaze narrowed at her tone and her choice of words. "Maybe I'm more than what the media makes me out to be. Does it matter who I am? To you?"

She glanced out at the gathering crowd and huffed. "Of course not. I just...thought you were a normal guy, buying trees as someone crazy about Christmas or as part of your job or something."

"It is part of my job. The resort needs to be decorated for the holidays."

"You *know* what I mean."

She was disappointed that he had money? Instead of fawning over him the way people—women—typically did because of his wealth, Sara apparently had an issue with it instead. But why?

Someone jumped onto the back of the truck and caused it to bounce a bit as the guys he'd commandeered from the hotel's maintenance and venue team began unloading the trees. "We'll continue this discussion later. Shall we?"

Rhys got out, ignoring the gawkers on the street not only taking in the activity but the fact he'd ridden in the truck rather than the Mercedes parked two car lengths away to give the guys space to unload.

As always, phones were pointed in his direction, and he ignored them as best he could while crossing round the front and holding Sara's door for her.

She emerged with a frowning glance at him before her gaze shifted to the crowd rapidly beginning to form, phones raised to stream and photograph and do all the things that meant privacy was a thing of the past.

Rhys gently grasped her elbow and escorted her out of the street to the sidewalk where Quinley and her best friend now waited, wearing jackets to offset the cool breeze blowing in off the ocean. Ana and Quinley were both engaged to Blackwell brothers, Cole and Elias respectively.

Both women were beautiful in their own way, but he suddenly realized they lacked the color and dark-haired fire he found so attractive in Sara.

He'd been blown away when Quinley left him at the altar last spring, but over the months since, they'd made it to the other side of the chaos and emotions. Somehow they'd remained friends. Close friends, much to Elias's irritation, and now the diamond engagement ring from Elias Blackwell sparkled in the sunlight as Quinley held the camera he'd requested.

"Sara Zinnick, I'd like to introduce you to Analise Taylor and Quinley Anders. Ana owns the Coastal Couture boutique inside the hotel, and Quinley handles PR for us here in Carolina Cove."

"And we're best friends, so sometimes when you call for one, you get us both," Quinley said with a smile. "Nice to meet you, Sara."

Sara stood stiffly beside him, cheeks rosy red beneath the glittery makeup. Her smile seemed tight.

"Nice to meet you both," Sara said.

"Shall we get started on pictures? Because *that* is a great costume, and the truck and trees." She blew a chef's kiss. "*This* is holiday magic right here. I can't wait to update the hotel's website and social media ads. We're running *way* behind on holiday enticement photos. I've been using stock photos that just aren't cutting it."

Sara looked even more uncomfortable.

"Don't worry. I'm pretty good at this—and you look fantastic. Seriously. Maybe just a few beside the truck for now? But more later when the trees are lit up and decorated," she hurried to add. "It would be *great* advertisement for the tree farm."

Rhys watched as Sara faltered, but the thought

of the photos helping her parents did the trick and lured her over her hesitation.

"I suppose a few would be okay," Sara said.

Rhys had one of the guys bring a tree to the side of the truck and cut the ties holding it closed. Unfurled, the tree was positioned so that the truck logo was visible, and Sara the elf smiled for the camera.

"Oh, these are *fantastic*," Quinley called. "Rhys, jump in there beside Sara. We need one of you both."

Sara swallowed, her smile wobbling as he did as ordered, with Quinley snapping away both with her phone and the professional camera she used.

"Perfect. These are awesome," Quinley said, showing the images to Ana who immediately agreed. "I'll create a few teasers to hint at something *big* going on at the hotel and then do a huge splash when everything is decorated and twinkly. Wait, grab the tree and take it to the other side. Let me get a few of you guys with the hotel as the backdrop. Santa's coming to town, after all."

Sara made to take the tree, but Rhys beat her to it. They repositioned on the other side, and Quinley had to wait for gawking traffic to crawl by before she could cross the street.

"Your ex...handles your PR?"

He glanced down at Sara's shorter, curvy frame and smiled. "We've both agreed we're much better as friends than we would've been as spouses. Please tell me you don't believe everything you see on the internet. Quinley is happily engaged, and I am happy for her. In fact, she and Ana will be sisters by marriage because they're marrying brothers."

Quinley made it to the other side and drew their attention by calling out instructions and snapping away. Had he given her more warning, she would've had a professional photographer there, but Quinley was quite a good photographer herself.

After a few minutes, Quinley called it a wrap for the time being. Rhys noted Sara visibly relaxed once it was over. "You don't like photos?"

Sara plucked at her costume and grimaced. "Not like this. This is more my mom's thing."

"Then I'll make sure Quinley gets some of you in regular clothes. You make a beautiful elf, though."

Sara met his gaze, cheeks flushed once more, and he found he quite liked the look on her.

Quinley joined them. Sara took a step back and turned to put some distance between them as they moved toward the sidewalk once more, but he caught her glance back over her shoulder. Once on the sidewalk, Quinley scrolled through the photos with feverish intensity while Sara shifted awkwardly.

The moment the last tree left the bed, Sara said, "They've finished unloading. I should go."

"No need to rush. Let me buy you lunch." Rhys ignored Quinley's quirking eyebrow as she pretended to focus on the camera and blatantly eavesdropped.

"Thanks, but I really should go," she said, making a move toward the cab of the truck. "I need to make a deposit and call about getting a new ship-ment of trees for the lot, and post a sign at the lot on when they'll arrive."

Rhys followed her back around to the driver's side and closed his fingers over the handle. "Fine. Go do what needs doing, but promise me you'll come back tonight."

"Why?"

Because he wanted her to; otherwise he'd have to find an excuse to visit a tree lot with no trees to buy. "We'll have some of the outdoor trees set up and lit by then, and we'll need more photos. I'll have Axel or the hotel's car service pick you up."

Sara's gaze flicked to the man in question. "He's your driver, not your boyfriend."

The comment earned a poorly disguised cackle from Quinley before Ana hushed her.

"You are correct," Rhys said, lips quirking. "We'll grab dinner after the photos."

Her head canted to the side. "Now it's dinner, too? Hasn't anyone ever said no to you before?"

"Not very often."

"That's a shame. It builds character," she said, waving a hand to indicate the truck door and the fact he was in her way and blocking traffic due to all the cars stopping to get a look.

He reluctantly opened the cab and watched once again as she climbed inside with a flash of striped elf leg. "Have it your way. We'll just have to use all the photos from today of you in costume if you don't come back to take more. Like Quinley said, it'll be good advertisement for your parents' business."

Sara frowned at him, her small hands clenching over the large steering wheel, a disgruntled expression on her freckled, glittery, beautiful face.

"Fine, I'll come back. But only because I hate wearing these in photos."

He grinned at her. "Perfect. I'll send a car for you at seven. See you then, Sara."

He stepped back and shut the door with a gentle slam, moving to the sidewalk as she started the truck and put the vehicle in gear. It rumbled away, and he watched until she was out of sight.

"Rhysand Xavier Lachlan," Quinley drawled in a low, *knowing* voice.

He gave her an innocent glance and shoved his hands into his pockets. "Yes?"

Quinley's gaze narrowed on him until she reminded him of the old schoolmarms seen in classic movies.

"You *like* her."

He glanced around, but now that the trees and the truck were gone, the crowd had thinned, and no one was close enough to hear her words. "I am... intrigued."

Her grin widened, and Quinley shot a look at her best friend before turning back toward him. "Oh, we can tell."

"You can?"

Quinley flipped the camera around and showed him a photo she'd taken of them when they weren't posed but just standing there, staring at one another as though neither of them could look away.

"See what I mean?"

Chapter Eight

Once she'd made the deposit and got back to the camper, Sara changed her mind a million times on whether or not to call up the hotel and leave a message for Rhys, cancelling the car service and the evening. At least her part in it.

Sara shoved the laptop off her lap onto the couch and glared at the clock, stomach churning when she remembered asking billionaire-heir Rhys Lachlan if his money was *real*. And then? Checking every bill to make sure it wasn't counterfeit—in front of him.

She groaned and covered her face with her arms as she leaned back into the pillow behind her. The Lachlan family was world-renowned for their business acumen and success, and she'd insulted the man while dressed as a *raccoon*.

She'd read the amusement on his face, but now her ignorance and question took on a whole other level of embarrassment.

And today? The photos?

Standing next to him with every breath bringing with it the tantalizing scent of his cologne, feeling the way she fit against his side, his arm around her shoulders tugging her closer. And then closer.

She'd struggled to smile, to breathe normally. Because that man?

There was a reason he'd made the sexiest-man list repeatedly. Men like him could get whatever they wanted. Whomever they wanted.

So why her? He'd flirted with her despite the stupid costumes and—*why*? She knew her number. She was a solid six on a good day. And that was being generous. Rhys was a fifteen on that same scale of ten. Seemingly a nice guy but so far out of her farm-girl league. She was a deeply rooted Christmas pine while he was a shooting star in the galaxy above. Something to be seen and admired from a distance.

She'd done some research after working on the story design she'd started a few weeks ago. Read the articles about his ex and their breakup. She'd even watched the video of Quinley Anders *hanging* over a penthouse balcony to make her escape on her wedding day.

Yet they still worked together on projects, like today, and Quinley's fiancé's restaurant was housed *inside* Rhys's hotel?

It was...odd. Like, seriously weird. Wasn't it?

Or was it an endgame play by Rhys to take his power away when and how he wanted to bring Quinley and her ex down? A power play he waited to deploy to destroy them at the most opportune moment? Because the uber-rich did things like that, didn't they?

Her phone rang, and she lowered her arms to see who called, body tensing even more as she answered. "Hey, Dad. How's Mom?"

"She's doing great. Every day is a little better," her father said. "Saralyn, what's with the bank deposit? Is that a mistake? And Buck said you called to get more trees delivered?"

"It's not a mistake, and I did call about more trees. I didn't say anything last night because I wasn't sure the customer would return today, but—I had a buyer come in last night and take every tree."

"*All* of them?"

"Yeah. And this morning he even brought help to

load them, so all I had to do was drive the truck to deliver them to the hotel. They're going to be displayed. I was about to call you, to check in and ask about visiting Mom since Buck said it would be a few days before he could get here."

Her father relayed the news to her mother, and Sara could hear her mother's groggy response in the background.

"And they're for a hotel?" he asked next.

"Yeah, the big new one. They had someone there to take pictures when I got there and... Actually they asked me to return tonight once some of them are decorated to do more photos, for social media. They...mentioned it would be good exposure for the farm."

"I'd say it would be by the looks of that deposit. You're going to go back, right?"

She glanced at the clock and frowned. "I thought I might cancel, actually. I just think it would be better if you were in the photos. Since Buck's going to be a few days, I could lock up and come stay with Mom while you take a break and come do the PR stuff."

"Ah, sweetheart, I know you want to see her, but that makes no sense. Besides, it's too expensive to do all that. I don't want to leave your mama either. I want you to go. If the lot's empty, you should get out and have some fun before you're tied down by the trees again."

She wrinkled her nose and rubbed a palm against her eyes. "It doesn't feel right. To have fun while you're both stuck in a hospital."

"Nothing will make me budge from your mama's side right now, and no one wants to see my old mug when they could see a pretty girl like you. Buck'll be working all weekend at the farm for the big Christmas event there, but I'll get him on the road as soon as it's over. Probably Tuesday or Wednesday. Thursday at the latest, but he'll be there before the weekend rush."

"That's fine, but are you sure I can't take the time to come visit Mama?"

"Booking a flight this late would cost the world, Sara. You can't afford it and neither can we. Wait until Christmas. When she's not sleeping due to the pain medicine, they've got her doing physical therapy or running more tests. Just wait until the season is over. She might be in the rehab place by then and up for company."

She hated that Mom was so far away but knew her father was right. She would be sitting around the hospital climbing the walls, or she could pitch in and do her part to actually help. "Okay, I'll wait. I guess I should go get ready for tonight. Give Mama a kiss for me."

"What costume you wearing for this one?" her father asked.

She bit back a groan. "No costume this time. Just regular clothes."

"Well, you'll represent us well either way," her dad said.

They hung up, and she pressed the button on her computer to save her work.

It was going to be a long time before her mom recovered enough to not need hourly care. She wasn't even out of the hospital yet, and while her father was great, he couldn't do it all. While she could use the time to send out résumés, she hesitated because she didn't know how long her family would need her.

Sara got up and went into the tiny camper bathroom. She'd changed out of the costume and washed her face as soon as she'd returned from the Lachlan Hotel, but when it came to going back this evening...

Professional was the way to go, she decided. She needed to showcase the other side of the coin, so to speak. Something opposite from the crazy costumes and fun family events on the farm.

She hadn't packed a cocktail dress with her when leaving in such a rush to take her parents' spot on the lot. But she *had* remembered how they were always invited to parties or gatherings by the local regulars, so she'd hastily thrown in a few dresses at the last minute, though at the time, she hadn't exactly known why since her parents were the ones who'd made the connections over the years, and it was doubtful the dresses would be needed.

She pulled the deep red, body-molding sweater dress—her one and only designer label that she'd picked up at a second-hand shop—over sheer thigh-highs, and then dug into the bottom of the suitcase for the heels with ankle bands.

Maybe it wasn't as fancy as a cocktail dress, but with her dark hair and olive complexion, she knew she looked nice.

She focused on her makeup, giving her eyes a bit of a winged appearance and adding a soft gloss to her lips. Out of time unless she wanted to be late, she ran a brush through her long dark hair and left it loose around her shoulders.

Nerves threatened to overtake her, but she shoved them off and reminded herself of the goal. Her parents desperately needed money to cover the hospital bills and rehab, and if a few photos would help the cause, and possibly get other hotels or businesses to notice them, who was she to argue?

A knock sounded at the camper door. Seven on the dot.

She grabbed her bag and coat and marched over, unlocking it to see a man in a dark suit on the other side. "Ms. Zinnick," he said with a dip of his head. "My name is Cole Blackwell, and I'm your driver for the evening. Are you ready to go?"

She frowned at the name. "Do you know Analise Taylor? I met her earlier today." Rhys employed yet another Blackwell? Weird just got weirder.

The man flashed a smile that lit his whole face, softening it. "She's my fiancée. We're getting married in the spring."

"Congratulations," she said, maneuvering the soft sand beneath her heels by shifting her weight to her toes.

Cole murmured his thanks and opened the rear door of the sleek town car, waiting patiently while she climbed inside. The ride to the hotel didn't take long, and a valet ran to open her door once they stopped.

She entered the beautiful new hotel, taking in the upscale furnishings and decor. This wasn't some run-of-the-mill beach motel but an honest-to-goodness resort that wowed.

"You look lovely, Sara."

She turned to face Rhys and watched as his gaze ran over her, feeling her body warm in response.

"I wondered if you'd cancel our date."

She blinked at his choice of words, heart stuttering at the heat in his gaze. "This is a photo opp. It isn't a date."

He gently took her elbow in hand to lead her toward a set of double glass doors. Outside she saw that some of the trees had been grouped and layered in varying heights and now twinkled with bright, sparkling lights. Giant lit gift boxes and oversized ornaments in pearl, teal, and gold lined the ground beneath.

"Hopefully by the end of the night it will be."

Chapter Nine

Rhys murmured the tantalizing words near her ear as he led her toward the tree display.

By the end of the thirty minutes spent taking photos with the professional photographer Quinley had arranged for the evening session, Rhys stared down at Sara's heart-shaped face and tried to pinpoint what it was about her that drew him so thoroughly.

She took his breath away in that dress, and he honestly wasn't sure why. She wasn't the most beautiful woman—though she was indeed beautiful—and she didn't have a model's thin lines or height.

Sara was shorter, curvier, *softer*, her dark hair tumbling around her neck and shoulders in finger-grabbing waves, her lips tinted with a lush nude gloss that continuously snagged his attention and left him fighting the urge to kiss her.

She *wasn't* his typical type, yet he couldn't take his eyes off her, something Quinley also seemed to notice if her amused, knowing gaze was anything to go by.

Like it or not, he couldn't help but compare the two women in question and realize they did share some similarities. Both were strong-willed and direct, characteristics he only now realized he preferred in a woman. So many ladies played the role of demure, anything-you-want airheads around him, and he hated it. He didn't want a doormat only interested in shopping, but he certainly didn't want someone pretending to be something they weren't. Some*one* they weren't.

These two? They were real and honest, though if *he* were honest, Sara's obvious and heartfelt, do-anything-for-family compassion drew him like a bee to a flower, and he wanted to know more. Know everything the background check hadn't provided. He'd put a rush on the inquiry, another thing that proved his interest was higher than normal.

Once the photos were finished, he escorted Quinley and Sara to the elevator for the ride up to

Haven. They made small talk about the photographer's upcoming show at a gallery, and when the elevator doors opened, Quinley stepped through first and walked into the waiting arms of her fiancé.

The two shared a quick yet blazing kiss, and Rhys caught Sara looking at him from beneath her lashes. He smiled down at her and placed a gentle hand at her back. "Shall we? My table's this way."

"Quinley isn't... I mean, I thought she was... joining us?"

The way Sara's face scrunched in confusion left him fighting the urge to kiss her once again. "No, she's joining her soon-to-be husband, now that the business stuff is completed. Is that a problem?"

Her chin jutted up at the question.

"No, it's just— Mr. Lachlan, what's going on?"

He chuckled at her formality, taking it as a sign he needed to slow his thoughts about her. Future billionaires didn't have a lot of time to date and therefore tended to skip a few steps and get straight to the gist of things. And while he'd read up on everything the background check had provided about her, Sara still saw him as someone she'd only just met. "Mr. Lachlan is my grandfather or my father. Call me Rhys."

"Okay. Rhys. What's going on?"

"Can you really not tell that I'm interested in you?"

He heard her shaky inhalation and reveled in the flush climbing from her neck to her cheeks.

"But *why?*"

"Why?" Could she not see what he saw? Her history had revealed her to be conscientious, hardworking, kind, compassionate. She'd dedicated herself to whatever job she'd worked—a perfect example being the tree lot she tended for her parents, all the while suffering and worrying due to her mother's accident.

"Yes, why? You're *you,* and I'm...not." She lowered her voice, her gaze sliding to the hostess stand where Quinley still stood. "I'm also not *her.* Or any of the other society women you've dated."

Rhys lifted his hand and gently brushed a stray strand of her inky dark hair from her cheek, lingering over the silky feel of her skin. "Maybe that's why I'm so intrigued. Have you considered that?"

Her blink told him he'd surprised her yet again. "This way, Sara. I'll introduce you to Elias later."

They left Quinley and Elias at the entry, and Rhys spotted the nervous hostess rushing toward them when she saw him leading Sara past the occupied tables toward the private area in the back.

The restaurant was crowded, and he was aware of the many eyes on them as he escorted Sara toward the windows. Her dark beauty drew admiring gazes along the way, and he knew before their dinner was over that word would spread.

"I'm sorry for the delay, Mr. Lachlan. Can I get you anything?" the hostess asked as she followed them to the table located behind a curving wall feature that allowed them privacy from the restaurant while giving them the perfect view of the coastline and Carolina Cove.

"You were busy, Lola. No need to fuss. And since I'm here practically every evening, I know the way to my table."

"Of course, sir. Enjoy your dinner."

Rhys watched as Sara slid into the luxuriously padded booth and settled before sliding in beside her rather than opposite. He noticed her fussing with the napkin and gently grasped her hand in his to still it. "Are you really so surprised by my interest?"

She blinked and nervously scanned the view before finally looking at him. "You're really okay with Quinley and her fiancé? Or is this," she glanced at their hands, "some kind of game?"

He supposed the question held merit, but coming from her in the tone she used... "Quinley and

I are over, though we've remained friends. I make a point of not missing out on good business opportunities due to personal biases, so when I heard how unique Elias's idea was, I wanted to be a part of it."

"Even though he's now engaged to your ex?"

"Even though," he said with a smile, fully aware that to a lot of people—his family included—the arrangement seemed strange. "Some people are better off as friends, and Quinley and I fall into that category. As to you... I give you my word. I'm not playing games."

She shook her head slightly as she inhaled.

"You don't believe me?"

"I don't know what to think."

"Then how about we talk and have a meal and get to know each other better? Then at the end of the night, decide if we want to do it again. Is that a reasonable request?"

She still looked uncertain, but he breathed easier when she finally nodded. "Good. So tell me about Sara."

Chapter Ten

Dinner was divine. The company too. And by the time it was over and they made their way to the elevator, Sara repeatedly told herself to get a grip because a tree farmer's daughter was *not* billionaire-heir material.

But right now, the way he looked at her?

It might not be a game, but you know whatever it is, it's temporary.

Instead of whisking them down to the ground floor, the elevator stopped after the shortest of rides, and the doors opened again.

She blinked at him but allowed him to tug her down a short hallway to a door. A swipe of his card opened into a glorious penthouse-floor suite. She stopped on the threshold. "Rhys..."

"No expectations, sweet Sara. I'll behave myself. But it's early yet, so I brought you here hoping we can try to find some of your missing Christmas spirit."

"How?" Yeah, she was suspicious. Especially since his promise to behave was said in a husky voice that curled her toes.

"By helping me decorate my tree?"

He pointed toward the interior, and she peered in to see one of the flocked trees she'd sold him freshly lit in the corner of the living space.

"I had my assistant get us some decorations. I thought we could decorate the tree, sip some wine and continue our conversation. What do you say?"

The lure of Rhys Lachlan should be bottled and sold. The combination of gorgeous man, gravelly voice and the sandalwood scent of his undoubtedly expensive cologne made for one heck of a heady elixir.

And while she had questions galore about why he paid her any attention at all, she lifted her chin and decided to gift herself this evening. After all, it wasn't every day she found herself on the receiving end of such a tantalizing man. And while he may be totally out of her league and more the fairytale prince to her forever-Cinderella-before-the-slipper, even Ella got a night at the ball. "I'm not sleeping with you."

Because there was fun—and then there was heartbreak. And if the last twenty-four hours had shown her anything, it was just how easy it would be to fall for someone like him. "You'll keep your hands to yourself."

His gaze warmed as she set the boundary, and she faltered at the sight. He looked at her as though... she'd passed some sort of test? That couldn't be right, though. Could it?

"Deal. Take your heels off and get comfortable," he said as he swept an arm wide to invite her inside. "This might take a while."

Two hours or so later, Sara stepped back and took in the glittering tree. Like the color scheme outside near the pool, the decorations provided were varying shades of beachy teals, golds, and pearly whites, but against the flocked tree, they stood out even more.

And since she was sort of a tree decorating expert after so many years on the farm, she willingly set the pace to keep her mind off her handsome host, rambling on about the best way to disguise gaps in the limbs and other nonsense. They inserted the largest ornaments or clusters of them into the bare spaces before working their way down to the smaller ones as fillers.

The majority of the decorations were bulbs, but there were also a few exquisitely beautiful seahorses, conches, and beach-themed items as well. Rhys's PA had even obtained a beautiful topper of faux sea oats, sparkling coral, and feathery *somethings* that she'd never have thought of as having potential in that grouping but looked absolutely stunning where it sat as the final piece to be added.

Rhys had found a music channel on the television, and holiday acoustic guitar played softly in the background. They took a break midway through and opened a delicious wine, sipping and chatting as they'd tucked and draped and fussed over each limb. She wore a bit of the fake snow on her dress, and Rhys had offered to get her a change of clothes, but she didn't mind. A quick wash and her favorite dress would be good to go again. That, and the thought of wearing Rhys's clothing was...more tempting than it should be.

She caught Rhys watching her again and like

every time before, her body warmed with a flush of awareness.

"Any plans of taking over your father's tree farm when the time comes?"

A low chuckle burst out of her as she shook her head. "The trees would die within a year." She wrinkled her nose. "I'm afraid I have a bit of a black thumb. Selling the trees is one thing, but growing them quite another."

She carefully secured a gold-and-glittery pearl-layered ribbon among the limbs and sighed. "I'm afraid in that aspect, I'm a huge disappointment to my parents. I've no doubt they hope I'll change my mind or marry someone interested in keeping up the tradition, but..."

"It's not the life you want?"

She pursed her lips and turned to grab another artfully tied ribbon. Wherever the decorations had come from, they weren't cheap. "The farm is great. It's...magical. I'm happy to visit and get my fix of fresh air and quiet, but...I also like coffee shops and busy streets."

"You could hire a manager to oversee things."

She smiled again, though this time it was pained. "Farms like my family's don't make much. They typically break even and do it for the love of it."

Sara caught Rhys's stare and sucked in a breath at the look in his gaze. "What?"

"Nothing. Just thinking. What was it like? Growing up there?"

He pulled story after story from her about her childhood and college years and parents' costumed antics and how much she hated that she couldn't be at the hospital to see her mother because she was needed to handle the lot.

Rhys distracted her with even more questions, and she reminisced about the good times of being a kid with so much room to run and play and explore. By the end, they were both laughing, with Rhys teasing her about being the love child of Santa and a raccoon.

"I think it's done," she said, having left the honor of placing the tree-topper to him and watching as he used his height and a stool to center it just right. "What do you think?"

He stepped down, but his foot caught on the edge of the stool, making him wobble.

She quickly steadied him even though he barely had to shift to adjust his weight to counter the stumble, but she saw his gaze warm as he used her instinct to "catch him" to pull her to him.

And like those photos taken earlier in the day,

she found herself breathing him in and staring up at his handsome face. "You said you'd...keep your hands to yourself."

He lowered his head, his intent clear, but stopped just shy of her lips.

"You touched me first."

"I suppose that did...break the rules."

"Mmm, it did," he agreed, his gaze lowering to her mouth. "May I kiss you, sweet Sara?"

She waited, unable to move or pull away, to do anything because she was so caught up in...this. Him. What better way than to end a wonderful evening than with a kiss?

She held his gaze and nodded. Because now? She didn't want the evening to end without one.

Rhys closed the distance between them but lifted his chin, his lips pressing gently against her forehead and lingering. The moment lengthened as her pulse pounded in her ears and she struggled to breathe. When he lifted his lips, she searched his gaze, seeing all sorts of heady, wonderful, thought-provoking things in the depths.

"Let's get you home," he said before adding, "before I'm tempted to do more than kiss you."

Rhys stepped back and released her. Sara watched, body tight and more than a little needy, as he took her hand and tugged her toward the couch where she'd left her shoes.

"As much as I don't want to end the evening, you need to get some rest before tomorrow."

She sat on the edge of the cushion to put her heels back on, but he followed her down, kneeling in front of her and taking her ankle in hand. She'd never considered watching a man buckle the straps around her ankle to be an erotic experience, but it was. "What's...happening tomorrow?"

First shoe finished, he lowered her foot to the floor before grasping the other ankle, lifting her foot to rest atop his knee while getting the other heel.

"You said you have a few days off while you wait on more trees to arrive. I'd very much like to spend them getting to know you."

She blinked at him, the light stroke of his fingers against her ankle and skin sending her pulse soaring. "You would?"

"I would. I'd like—"

Rhys suddenly stilled, and she followed his dark gaze to see the move had shifted her skirt an inch or two higher, riding up to reveal a peek of the lace trim at the top of her stockings. They landed midthigh, revealing nothing a pair of shorts wouldn't show, but the way he gazed at her... "Better than elf stripes?"

Rhys released a low growl. "Better than elf stripes."

He shifted his hand and lightly brushed his fingertips along the lace before withdrawing them. "Let's get you home, sweet Sara."

Chapter Eleven

Around ten the following morning, Rhys knocked on the camper door and waited for Sara to respond. He took in the empty lot, nodding toward the guard positioned down the road a bit but within sight.

According to his morning report, the empty lot still drew attention. The guard had run off two teenagers lurking around yesterday when Sara had driven the trees to the hotel, as well as a drunk who'd ridden in on a bicycle in the early hours of the morning who "just wanted to talk to the pretty woman staying there."

The camper door clicked and swung open, and he turned his attention to Sara.

He'd escorted her back to the camper last night

and left her after a kiss goodnight. He'd then dreamed of her deep red dress and lace-trimmed stockings.

Sara stood a step above him, which put her at his eye level. Unable to stop himself, he learned forward and brushed her lips with his, lingering over the caress but keeping things light. "Hi."

"Hi," she whispered back.

"Are you ready?"

"I am. I wish you'd tell me what we're doing though. Is this okay?"

He took in her jeans and low-heeled boots, topped by an oversized sweater that draped off one kissable shoulder. "You look perfect. But grab your coat just in case."

The temp was warm and pleasant for a December day. The kind of day where only a sweater was required.

He stepped back as she descended the camper step and locked up, and he took her hand and held it to his lips for a kiss before leading her toward the SUV where Axel waited.

Axel opened the passenger door for them as they approached, but Sara's attention locked on something elsewhere.

"What's wrong?"

"That guy—in the car over there. Do you see him? He was here yesterday morning. I thought he was waiting on someone then, but I told him we'd sold out of trees and wouldn't restock for a few days. I also saw Axel speak to him when you came to pay for the trees but— Why's he just sitting there?"

Rhys paused and prepared himself. "He's watching over you, Sara." He studied her expression, felt the way she tensed at the news.

"You put a *body*guard on me? Why?"

His ex-fiancée's voice filled his head, high-pitched and angry as Quinley had demanded he remove her security team and give her back her privacy. "I didn't like the idea of you here alone, and I wanted to make sure you were safe. And before you come at me, he's had to run a few people off, so please don't expect an apology."

She sucked in a breath at that bit of news, but he felt the truth needed to be told so she fully understood. Carolina Cove was a great little town, but she was a woman alone, a fact that had already been noted by the thieves and drunks and others paying attention.

"He's had to...do that?"

Rhys shoved his hands into his pockets and nodded. "Yes, he has. Look, Sara, I'm not trying to be creepy or controlling, but you're isolated, and I wanted to keep you safe. For my own peace of mind, if not yours."

She stayed silent a few beats.

"I can't pay you back."

"I'm not asking you to. I want to know you're safe. That's all I need."

"That's...kind of you, Rhys. Thank you. For watching out for me."

Surprise blew through him, and he canted his head as he stared down at her beautiful face. "You're taking the news better than I expected."

A low laugh rumbled out of her as she hugged her coat to her chest. "Well, I'd be lying if I said it wasn't creepy staying here at night, and... I had a stalker in high school. Nothing big but— some guy from another school. Thankfully we didn't have to call in the police because the guy listened when my father caught him on the farm and said no one would find his body if he kept coming around and scaring me."

"I like your dad."

"He's the best," she agreed. "So...while it's unexpected, thank you. The last thing my parents need is to be worrying about me should something happen, and they can't afford to hire anyone else or drag Buck away from the farm right now. Not that I want to share the camper with Buck."

"You will *not* be staying with Buck, whoever he is."

She released a throaty laugh at his grumble, and Rhys found himself relaxing at the sound. He thought he'd have a fight on his hands like he'd always had with Quinley, but Sara had rolled with the news with a grace and acceptance he admired. "And you're very welcome. Shall we get going?"

"Are you going to tell me *where* we're going?"

He grinned down at her as he wrapped his arm around her shoulders and pulled her to his side, lips pressing a kiss to her hair. "It's a surprise."

It took minimal time to get to the marina at this time of day, and Rhys smiled at Sara's shock when Axel rolled up to the dock.

"We're taking a boat?"

"Do you get seasick? I was told the captain has antinausea meds on board, just in case."

She shook her head and gathered her things, excitement rolling off her as they exited.

Rhys led her toward their charter for the day and reveled in the grin she couldn't wipe from her face, amused by how her head whipped from side to side as she tried to take everything in at once.

Over dinner at Haven, Sara had mentioned loving the hamburgers from the Cohens' pier house, so he'd placed an order for their trip. His PA had tried to handle the details and do something "nicer," and normally Rhys would've let him, but this felt different. Because Sara felt different, and he wanted to plan the day on his own.

Still, Axel carried their special lunch and followed them to the boat.

The captain quickly got them underway, and they headed south down the Intercoastal Waterway.

The wind picked up with their speed, and both donned their coats before moving to the railing. Sara took a few photos on her phone. She then slid it back into her pocket and glanced up at him.

"Having fun?" he asked.

"You know it," she said, smiling at him. "I haven't been on a boat in years. Is it yours?"

"No, I leave the boat buying to my father."

She tilted her chin up as she turned sideways to lean against the rail. "And you won't tell me where we're going?"

"We're recapturing your Christmas spirit."

A hesitant expression formed on her features, and he frowned. "What's wrong? Why the look?"

"It's just— You don't have to spend money on

me. You know that, right? I mean this is *wonderful,* but you've already done too much."

"What do you mean?"

"Buying the trees and helping my parents. Then the guard. Now this?"

He moved behind her and wrapped his arms around her. "The trees were business—with helping your parents out a nice bonus. The guard for my peace of mind, like I said. And the boat— I'm selfish, Sara. This is for me as well. I can go very few places and have privacy. Stealing you away for the day without having cameras pointed at us protects us both."

She stiffened a bit in his arms, and he frowned. "What?"

"Nothing."

"Sara? Talk to me. Please."

She avoided his gaze and looked out at the sparkling water and coastal homes rolling by.

"Is it the media attention?" He couldn't blame her. He hated being hounded for quotes and photos or interviews. "Things have calmed down considerably since spring, but I'm afraid that's an aspect of my life that won't change."

He couldn't read her expression, but something made him think that wasn't it. At least not all of it.

"Let's just enjoy the beautiful day."

Yeah, something still bothered her. He could tell by the tight lines of her body and the way her eyebrows scrunched over her nose in an adorable furl. But she refused to share whatever thought had set her on edge, so he let it go for the moment. Maybe the day would loosen her thoughts and whatever the worry was.

He pressed his lips to soft skin and kissed away the frown. "We're almost there."

"*Where?*"

He chuckled at her grumbly tone. "You'll see."

Chapter Twelve

There was an isolated strip of sand along Masonboro Island. They'd taken their time getting to the spot and arrived around noon.

The captain slowed the boat and threw the anchor before Sara and Rhys boarded a tiny dinghy to get to shore.

Axel stayed behind with the captain, but she noted the man had given Rhys a two-way radio as well as a picnic basket before their departure.

The basket looked like something off the set of a Hallmark movie, right down to the red-and-white-check cloth artistically draped over the top.

"Walk a bit and eat?"

She stared at him, more than a little taken aback

by the thought that Rhys seemed to *like* this sort of thing. Was it possible? He'd promised no games but — A picnic on a private stretch of beach? "Sounds good."

They stayed until the sun sank deep into the sky and lit it on fire. The deep purples and reds spread out like a blanket and cast a haze over the homes as they made their way back to the marina.

They'd spent the day strolling along the sand after eating their lunch, and she wasn't sure what surprised her more. The fact that Rhys hadn't ordered something from an expensive restaurant like Haven or that he'd actually *listened* to her when she'd rambled on while decorating his Christmas tree about how she loved the burgers and onion rings from the Cohen's pier house.

Maybe she was the judgy one when it came to Rhys, but she'd never pictured a billionaire-heir eating paper-wrapped, loaded burgers and agreeing on how awesome they were.

They'd walked for hours. Literally hours. They'd just walked and talked and eventually filled the basket to the brim with seashells she couldn't bring herself to leave behind. Thankfully angel shells were light, but they'd found a lot of them, and she couldn't wait to take them to her mother. Her mother loved crafting in the off-season months, and angel shells were her favorite. She'd glue them together and add tiny faces and glitter and pearls and other adornments to make the most beautiful ornaments to sell in the gift shop at the farm.

When she'd told Rhys her reason for gathering them, he'd insisted she get all that she wanted, even going as far as to contact the boat via the radio and have Axel meet them to exchange the full basket for empty buckets to hold them all.

She'd laughed at Rhys's determination to get her mama perfect shells, and then they competed to find the most before picking up a few sun-bleached welks, lion's paws and scotch bonnets. She found four palm-sized sand dollars, a few smaller ones, and a tiny starfish.

By the time they headed back to the boat, her feet were dragging and her face hurt from smiling so much. Rhys's stories about growing up running wild in the many hotels his family owned had left her teary from laughter. Apparently laundry shoots and off-limits areas were his favorite places, and avoiding hotel security was quite the game.

They held hands, and each carried a bucket topped with shells. Rhys had even stuck a few of the larger, heavier ones in the front pocket of his hoodie.

But the closer they came to the dinghy for the return trip, the slower she walked. She couldn't help it. It had been the perfect day, and she didn't want it to end.

Reality bit the big one, and her reality was that this happy bubble would inevitably burst because they had nothing in common.

She didn't come from money or have an Ivy League education. She didn't know the who's who among the society set. She wasn't rich and her bank account lacked far too many of the zeros needed to get remotely close.

This perfect day was just that...a day to hold onto in the future when Rhys would meet someone who better fit his status.

Because even if she could handle the spotlight of the media he tried to avoid, who was to say he wanted the tree farmer's daughter at his side when those photos were taken?

Was that the *real* reason he'd brought her way out here? So no one would see them on their "date"?

She thought about the private booth in Haven where he'd seated her. How he'd taken her back to the penthouse alone to decorate the tree. Now this. And, yes, maybe she was overthinking everything because she was tired from their busy day, but *what if* the reason Rhys did all those things was because he liked something about her but was...embarrassed of her? Of her background and upbringing and all the things that made her *her*?

"Have I worn you out?"

She grasped onto the excuse with both hands and nodded. "Yes, but I think we found enough shells to keep my mom happy for years."

His low chuckle sent a warm feeling through her, and she handed over her bucket when he moved to take it. He carried them to the dinghy and pushed it out, then turned back toward her once more, swinging her up in his arms to keep her feet dry. He settled her onto the seat with a kiss brushed over her lips before he climbed in to get them on their way to the boat.

The roar of the outboard motor made it difficult to talk, but the ride to the anchored boat was quick. Once back on board, Rhys left the captain and his one-man crew to secure the dinghy and followed her to her new position at the railing. "Come here, sweet Sara."

He stood at her back and wrapped his arms around her, hugging her close. Sara closed her eyes, turning her nose into his sweatshirt to breathe in the scent of soap and man and tangy salt air. Such a heady, knee-weakening combination.

Rhys eventually lured her back to the seating area. He'd offered to take her below out of the wind, but she didn't want to miss a moment of the ride back or the last rays of sunshine.

The air chilled as the sun set, and she leaned closer to his side, basking in the warmth he shared as she curled into him. The final rays faded, and darkness closed in as they slowly trolled back to the marina.

It really was the perfect day. But she knew all good things came to an end.

Chapter Thirteen

The following morning, Rhys looked up from where he browsed inside Coastal Couture and found Ana and Quinley both staring at him with inquisitive expressions. "What?"

Quinley smirked. "I take it your business dinner turned out well? I tried to drop off the samples from the photos, and Paul said you'd cleared your schedule for the next few days."

He canted his head, and figured at this point, he deserved the ribbing for the hard time he'd given her in regards to Elias right after their breakup. "Shouldn't you be working or upstairs with your fiancé?"

"I came to see my best friend," she countered. "Why are *you* here?"

"I need a gift," he said simply.

"For Sara?" Quinley pressed.

"Not for Sara." He watched the best friends exchange a glance. "Could you wrap this up for me, Ana?" He pointed at the miniature tree with its sparkling adornments.

"Of course. Which one do you want?"

He smiled, knowing his response would pique their interest even more. "All of them. And the tree."

The display had immediately drawn his attention as he'd walked by because dangling from the limbs were tiny, glittery gemmed trinket boxes. No two were alike, but there was a tree, Santa and Mrs. Claus, a porcupine, a fairy, a dark-haired elf and his favorite—a raccoon with a red bow at its neck.

Sara had mentioned her mother wearing her colorful costumes on the farm, and the customers not knowing if they'd be greeted by a fairy or animal. And since her mother's hospital had also been listed in the background report he'd had done on Sara, and the figurines might brighten her mother's day... "Can you ship them as well? I'll text you the address. All but this one. I want to take it with me."

"Sure. I'll wrap it separately and send an invoice

once I get the shipping cost," Ana said as she took the raccoon from him and quickly moved to the checkout.

Quinley hadn't stopped staring at him, and he shoved his hands into his pockets as he waited for her interrogation.

He didn't have to wait long.

"It looks good on you."

"What does?" he asked, unsure of what she meant since it wasn't what he'd expected her to say.

"Sara-dust. I don't remember you ever looking so...happy."

"Quinley..."

"I *mean* it. You've found the missing something, haven't you?"

In their first face-to-face conversation after she'd left him at the altar, they'd both admitted to something missing from their relationship. Something important.

Had he found it with Sara? It certainly felt that way. He might not have known her long, but he'd never felt as relaxed or intrigued or *in want* of a woman in his entire life, not even for the one in front of him who'd done them both a favor by balcony diving to get away from him the day of their almost wedding. "I've only just met her."

"When it's real, you know it. I knew with Elias. Maybe not immediately, but...I knew. There was that *something* that made him different."

"Elias-dust?" he asked with a smirk and lift of his eyebrow.

Quinley laughed and nodded. "Elias-dust, yes. Make fun if you like, but I see you, Rhys Lachlan. You've got a sparkle in your eye." She smiled again. "It looks good on you."

He held her gaze, thinking she was right considering he'd spent the entire night dreaming of a certain windblown, dark-haired beauty.

He'd had so much fun doing nothing but strolling the beach with her, picking up shells. Sneaking kisses and loving her triumphant grins when she'd one-up him in their shell competition.

He'd struggled to take her home, wanting, praying, she'd invite him into the tiny camper to stay even if it meant keeping his hands to himself.

He hated the thought of not sleeping beside her, waking up beside her every day, and he wanted to do all he could to give her the life she deserved.

But the suddenness of it? He wasn't a man who made impulsive decisions, though in this he felt like his mind was already made up. He knew it was crazy. But that's how he felt.

"Here you go," Ana said, bringing him a beauti-fully wrapped package.

He blinked, so distracted by his thoughts he'd nearly forgotten about the gift. "Thanks."

"I'll get everything ready to send out as soon as you text the shipping address. Do you need help with anything else?"

Last night, he'd reminded himself of the endgame and escorted Sara to the camper, backing her up against the side and kissing her senseless until they were both breathing heavily. When she'd finally pulled away, it seemed like she struggled just as much as he did with the chemistry and feelings over-taking them.

He prided himself on his ability to see things logically and objectively, but he could see no down-side here.

Some might think he needed to marry a wealthy socialite or secure some sort of business arrangement to better his position and gain power, but he couldn't care less about that.

He did well; he had enough money for several lifetimes. Would inherit more. He wanted something real, something lasting. "I think that's it. Have a good day, ladies."

Rhys left the store with the pretty package, and Axel fell into step behind him outside the boutique.

They made their way through the hotel, drawing attention as always from guests and employees alike.

Rhys focused on Sara. On his next steps.

When they'd headed back to the boat, he'd sensed her withdrawing from him. That lasted all the way back to the camper when she'd ended the make-out session, even though he'd sensed her own reluctance.

She'd looked wide-eyed and more than a bit unsteady on her way inside the camper, her response as precious to him as the potential of what might be if Quinley was right about *Sara-dust*.

Chapter Fourteen

The days before Christmas passed in a blur. The last two days of freedom before the new shipment of trees arrived were spent with Rhys. He came to the camper every day to pick her up, and they'd go for a drive or grab lunch or just go back to the hotel suite to watch the classic Christmas movies he insisted she needed to see in order to recapture the Christmas spirit she'd claimed to lack.

She'd had more fun and laughed more since meeting her handsome new friend than she had in ages, but with every hour that passed in seclusion with him, the doubt that niggled at her about him being embarrassed of her grew. And grew some more.

She allowed herself to enjoy her time with him. Gave herself over to the tantalizing kisses and the breathless sighs he drew from her before she forced herself to stop the madness, believing it would avoid the heartbreak she saw looming in the days ahead.

She knew it wouldn't stop that tug of pain, but keeping herself from taking that last step was critical in her mind. A last-ditch effort to avoid worse pain should she succumb.

Now it was her last evening of freedom. Buck would arrive with a load of trees tomorrow, and her time with Rhys would end as abruptly as it began. But maybe it would help break the addiction that was Rhys Lachlan and clear her muddied brain from wanting more than she could expect to have.

She liked herself. She was a smart, capable woman. She loved and was loved by friends and family. She was confident in her talents and abilities as a human being. But she *knew* her level in the scheme of life, and whatever this was with Rhys wouldn't last. It wasn't *real*.

She'd allowed herself a few days to revel in the excitement and headiness of Rhys, but when it came down to it?

She wanted a fireplace. She wanted that warm,

safe, hot pleasure that could be stoked high or banked, but would never, ever burn out.

It was what her parents had, and it was what she craved in her very soul. She couldn't count the times her parents had embarrassed her with their PDAs. But anyone with eyes and ears knew without any doubt they *loved,* and they loved deeply. Even after all their years together, the fireplace still burned.

This thing with Rhys was a firework. It was hot and heady and beautiful in all its blazing, sparkly glory, but it would explode and fizzle and be gone in the blink of an eye. Burned out and forgotten as the next firework flared to life for him.

They'd planned to spend the final day together, but Rhys had business he had to handle that couldn't wait, so she'd spent the morning working on her children's story and making notes for the pages she'd need to design.

When she'd nearly given up on seeing him, he'd texted that he was finished and on his way. No doubt for another evening shielded from everyone like a secret.

She blinked, realizing she just stood there staring down at her clothes strewn across the camper bed and wasn't making progress on finding a "last date" outfit. She grabbed a deep emerald sweater and paired it with jeans before adding booties and decided it worked.

Since it was windy outside, she pulled her hair into a sleek pony and hurried through makeup, focusing on her eyes and lips. No matter what, though, she couldn't shake the thought that of all the time they'd spent together, they'd never really gone out in public. A business dinner hidden from view of the restaurant guests after the photo session didn't count.

She'd just finished when a knock sounded on the camper door and sent her pulse racing. She put her feet in motion, pulling the little divider closed so whoever it was couldn't see her pitiful selection of clothes scattered across the bed.

She unlocked the door and pushed it open to see Rhys standing on the other side.

"Sweet Sara," he said in that husky tone, his gaze sweeping over her and heating her blood to boiling in an instant. "May I come in?"

She eyed his jeans and black button-down shirt beneath a sleek black leather coat, relaxing a bit at her clothing choice for the evening, and stepped back. "Um—there's not a lot of room in here."

He filled the tiny space and pulled the door closed behind him. The overhead light cast shadows over his dark hair and handsome face, and she watched as his gaze took in the kitchenette, dinette table and bench, and the bathroom. Her parents left colorful string lights up year-round, but there was little clutter otherwise.

Still, it was the perfect example of her life versus his. Another reminder of just how very different they were. The thought made her heart wither a little more. "Not quite the penthouse, huh?"

His gaze shifted from place to place, and she watched and waited, wondering at his thoughts when he remained quiet. After another moment, she began to squirm.

"You don't have a Christmas tree even though you sell them?"

The question pulled a nervous huff from her, and she tucked her fingers into her rear pant pockets to keep from wringing them like a rag. "My mom usually does, but—I haven't bothered with it."

"I thought the last few days had helped you find some of that missing holiday spirit," he murmured, his gaze locking on hers.

The heat she spied in his eyes left her belly fluttering even as her heart shriveled up that final inch. She'd forgotten about Rhys's determination to bolster her flagging holiday spirit. He'd considered it a challenge, and if she'd learned nothing else about him, he took on challenges with his mind set to win them.

She'd made it all too easy, lapping up every ounce of his attention like Cinderella sweeping up all those ashes.

"We should fix your tree situation."

"The new load will be here tomorrow. I'll have more trees than you can shake a candy cane at." She pointed to the table. "I'll snag one and put it there. It's fine."

"Good. Until then, you can put this on the table. But no opening it until Christmas."

He stuck a hand in the pocket of his jacket and pulled out a beautifully wrapped package.

"You bought me a present?"

"Just a little something that reminded me of you."

She sank her teeth into her plump lower lip and hesitantly took the gift he still held out for her. "Thank you, but you shouldn't have. I know you're... I know you're trying to boost my holiday spirit, but I don't expect gifts."

His expression warmed and softened, and the sight of it left her breathing shallow.

"Sweet Sara, let's go have fun, yeah?"

It seemed important to him and because it was her last day before chaos descended and her time with him disappeared like that burst of crackling firework, she nodded. "Yeah."

Chapter Fifteen

Rhys decided that evening that he was indeed a very selfish man. The business meetings he'd had to get through earlier that day had been with Everett Drake.

Research had shown Rhys that Drake's beautiful wife, Isabel, and Sara had more than a few things in common, so when Drake had issued a dinner invitation for the future, he'd countered with getting together that very evening.

He wasn't a patient man, and he felt his time with Sara slipping through his fingers. She'd want to leave Carolina Cove the moment the lot closed, to go be with her parents in their time of need—as she should—but he didn't want the decision to be easy for her.

The evening went well, though he'd sensed Sara's nervous panic when they'd first arrived at the couple's seaside home.

Sara had shot him a few daggers when he'd explained the situation, and he'd apologized for the short notice and not telling her sooner, but he also wasn't sorry since he hadn't wanted Sara to worry over dinner with strangers.

As he'd suspected, Sara and Isabel instantly hit it off, and after dinner, they'd settled in to chat about art and design since Isabel was an up-and-coming painter. He boldly eavesdropped, listening to Sara shyly explain her desire to write and illustrate children's books.

"Not your usual type, from what I understand."

Drake's low murmur as he prepared to make his next play on the billiard table drew Rhys's attention back to the man. "So I've been told."

Everett smirked and nailed the shot. "She and Isabel have a lot in common. Smart move bringing her to meet and see how it can be done."

Rhys grunted out a sound but never took his eyes off the ladies. "Am I that obvious?"

"Only to someone who's been there."

Rhys shifted his attention to the man across the table from him. "Any advice?"

Everett snagged the chalk and focused on his pool cue. "You can give her whatever she wants, but if she's anything like Isabel, what she wants is the real man. That's what makes them both terrifying and perfect."

A low chuckle rumbled out of Rhys at the man's words, and he nodded. Sara wasn't artificial, and Drake's words reenforced his own thoughts about her.

After a few games and a nightcap, Rhys and Sara left the Drakes's before their infant son's bedtime and headed to the hotel, Sara snuggled against his side for the short ride.

Everett's words resonated in Rhys's mind as they quietly discussed their dinner hosts. Rhys escorted Sara through a side entrance and used a service elevator to avoid being seen.

Inside his suite, he left the lights dimmed low so that the tree was the main focus, sparkling from the corner. "You and Isabel seemed to be fast friends."

Sara smiled and nodded as he settled in beside her on the couch to pull her close for the Christmas movie she'd chosen.

"She's amazing. She showed me her art studio and her current work, and even invited me to her upcoming show in January."

He'd received an invitation for the private show-case as well and made a mental note to accept. "I'd be happy to escort you."

Something in her expression darkened, like the light went out of her gaze before she averted her eyes. "Did I say something wrong?"

"No. Not at all."

"Sara. What is it?"

"It's nothing. Really. I just—don't know where I'll be in January." She shook her head and gave him a sad smile. "I'm...enjoying our time together. Let's not burst the bubble until we have to, okay? Can we just..."

She waved a hand toward the television and the tree, and he understood her meaning clear as day.

She thought this was temporary. That they were merely passing time as two lonely people by them-selves near the holidays. And while he wanted to protest her thinking and shower her with reassur-ances, he also knew coming on too strong wouldn't serve him because she'd balk and say he wasn't sincere.

His sweet Sara was complicated in that way.

But since actions were more powerful than words, he drew her to him and covered them with a cozy blanket, pressed Play and silently promised her the future he intended to create for them.

Sara opened her eyes with a lazy blink and pressed her nose to the deliciousness beneath her. So good. Like whiskey and salt and—

"Good morning, sweet Sara."

She swallowed. How could anyone sound and *smell* so good in the morning? And it was morning, given the way the sunlight streamed into the suite.

She didn't want to move, and when she tried, she found herself trapped between the back cushions of the couch and Rhys's long, hard body.

"We fell asleep." She croaked like a thirsty frog and cringed. No sexy, throaty morning voice for her.

"We did. Best night's sleep I've had in a very long time."

His fingers tightened in her hair before relaxing and rubbing softly, the move making her eyes close in pleasure.

"Mmm. Keep looking like that and I'll never let you leave."

His lips suddenly pressed to hers in a kiss that was soft and heady and all things tantalizing. So much so she forgot about morning breath and the slight headache from lack of coffee.

"What do you want for breakfast? Or lunch? We slept in, and I didn't want to wake you."

The realization that it was lunch time jolted through her. That and the fact he'd apparently been lying there trapped by her and watching her sleep. Who did that? "What time is it? I have to get to the lot. Buck was supposed to be there by ten."

"It's nearly eleven."

"Oh, no. I can't believe I slept so late. Why didn't you wake me up?"

"You obviously needed the rest, sweetheart. We've had some busy days, and you've been writing and designing instead of resting."

She tried to scramble up and struggled, given the way she was pinned between him and the couch, the two forming a steady, warm, heavy blanket of safety. No wonder she'd slept so well.

Rhys got up and then helped steady her as she finally swung off the couch to her feet. She flushed when he gently patted down her bedhead and gently ran his thumbs under her eyes.

"Perfect."

He kissed her again before she pulled away for a

quick trip to the bathroom. One glance in the mirror above the sink proved that while she did look rough from sleeping in her makeup, she did appear better rested.

She rinsed her mouth with water, finger-brushed her hair even more and headed out to be on her way home.

Rhys waited, looking like he'd splashed his face somewhere else in the suite if his spiky lashes were any indication.

"Are you ready?"

"You don't have to come with me."

"A gentleman sees his date home." He tilted his head toward the door, and they left, once again using the service elevator.

Downstairs, Axel waited at the side of the building. She was quickly tucked into the vehicle, and they were on their way to the lot in seconds.

Like she'd feared, Buck waited for her to show up. The thirty-something man scowled when he saw her get out of the back of the fancy Mercedes, and Sara flushed when Buck gave them both a once over, like he could tell they'd spent the night together. Even though nothing had happened other than a few kisses during the movie.

"Hi, Buck. Thanks for bringing the new load."

"You okay, Sara? I got worried when you didn't answer. I even called a few times."

Sara refused to look at Rhys. "I'm fine. My phone died, and— The trees look great. I'm sure they'll sell well."

Buck continued to glare at Rhys, who stared right back. She glanced between them, finally realizing the two were engaged in a silent battle for dominance.

Buck had liked her for years, but she'd never returned his feelings. And while she and Rhys weren't really a couple, both men shot daggers as though staking a claim. "Rhys, this is Buck, my dad's farm manager. Buck, this is Rhys."

Rhys's hand slid up her back to her neck where he gently but firmly squeezed in a gentle massage.

"Nice to meet you, Buck."

Buck dipped his head but didn't return the greeting.

"Well, Buck, I appreciate you unloading them and getting things set up. I'm sure you want to get back on the road."

"I can stay the night and pitch in. I'm sure you'll be busy once people see the lot is restocked."

"No need," Rhys said. "I'll help her."

She jerked her head toward him and saw Rhys

still stared at the other man. "You'll...*help* me? Sell Christmas trees?"

Rhys finally broke his glare to look at her, amusement in his gaze at her audible surprise.

He used his hold on her to tug her close enough to drop a kiss to the top of her head and murmur, "Of course, sweet Sara. I am at your service."

Chapter Sixteen

That's not a tree, Sara."

"It's perfect. It's...whimsical."

Thirty minutes later, after seeing a visibly upset Buck back on the road toward the farm, they stood inside the tiny camper staring at the *limb* Sara had chosen as her tabletop tree.

There were prettier ones among those available outside, and he didn't know if she simply didn't want to take a better tree from those provided or if it was a sympathy thing. He leaned toward believing it was Sara's soft heart that did the choosing for her.

She'd seen the tree and instantly veered toward it. The smallest tree there, it fell over at the top like the Drakes' tired toddler draped across his father's shoulder. "Sara..."

"Rhys," she said in the same tone.

He watched as she crossed her arms over her chest and angled her head to stare up at him, determination and fire in her beautiful eyes.

"It's my camper and my tree. I get to pick."

He couldn't argue that. "Fine. Have it your way. But you know one ornament might make it fall over."

A giggle burst out of her, and his heart warmed at the sound. This woman...

"Good thing I just want lights on it then, huh?"

Exasperated and yet willing to go along with whatever made her smile, he stretched out a hand and palmed her face, holding her still for a firm kiss. "Have it your way. But since the present is nearly as big as the tree, I want you to go ahead and open it."

"Now? You said I had to wait."

"I changed my mind. Open it." He watched as she held the package in one hand and carefully unwrapped the box. "It reminded me of you, beautiful and sparkling and unique."

A soft *oooh* bubbled out of her when she spied the gemmed raccoon. At least until a second passed and her expression faltered.

"The perfect keepsake to remind me of the humbling moment I asked *you* if your money was real."

He frowned at her tone, at the shift in expression from pleased and surprised to...disgruntled as she stared at the gift. "Do you not like it?"

"It's very pretty," she said, her tone forced.

He stretched out a hand and stroked his fingers across her cheek. "I couldn't take my eyes off of you that night."

Sara blinked and inhaled before shifting her gaze to stare up at him. "Rhys..."

She sounded uncomfortable, and once again, he could see her physically withdrawing from him. But why? "The gift isn't expensive if that's what you're worried about."

"It's not."

"Then what's wrong?"

A huff left her, full of recriminations and sadness. "It just—reminded me of how different we are. Opposites. And how none of this is real."

He frowned at her words, taken aback by the vehemence behind them. "What do you mean?"

"This. Whatever *this* is, whatever's happening between us... It's *not* real. I-I think I need to stop this before it's too late. It's time we both remember who we are. That I remember who *you* are."

He stepped toward her, but she backed away

from him, shaking her head, fingers white over the raccoon in her hand.

"I'm sorry, Rhys. You should go. I-I can't keep pretending in fairytales o-or that this is more than you...passing time."

"Passing time? You think that's all this is?"

"Isn't it?"

"You're seriously that *biased* against me? Because I'm rich? Sara, I've worked hard to have what I have, and that's with*out* my family's wealth."

"I'm not arguing that."

"But you think what's happening between us isn't real because of who I am? That I'm somehow less deserving of love because I have money?"

"No!"

"Then what is this really about? The truth, Sara."

The way she stared into his dark gaze broke his heart, and Rhys fisted his hands at the expression on her face. "*Sara.*"

"Do you really think I can't tell?" She swallowed hard and lifted her chin higher, eyes glazed with tears. "You're ashamed to be seen with me."

He felt like his knees might buckle from the anger coursing through him. "That *isn't* true."

"Isn't it? I googled you, and I saw all the photos

of you with your— Of you with the women you've dated. But me? You've hidden me from the beginning. We take the service elevator to your suite where we stay in, and you took me to a remote beach just so you weren't seen with me. And I get it. I'm the tree farmer's daughter, and you're *you*. We are *worlds* apart when it comes to literally everything. So why are you pretending? You want to sleep with me? Is that it?"

"I'm not ashamed of you, Sara. I'm trying to *protect* you. Do I want to be with you? Yes, of course. You're a beautiful woman, but that's not— If we're seen together, the media will hound you from that moment on. They will invade every aspect of your life. I am *not* embarrassed of you, sweetheart; I am simply trying to keep you safe and to myself for as long as I possibly can because I don't want to share you."

She looked wary and highly skeptical, more than a little taken aback by his words as she remained quiet for long seconds. He inched closer, lifting his hands to cradle her face so that she wouldn't look anywhere but at him. "The very moment I saw you, something clicked. I don't believe in love at first sight, but I do know I felt *something* that night, something I've never felt and all for this beautiful...*raccoon*," he said, smiling at the memory.

Her gaze sparkled with unshed tears as she stared up at him, her expression flashing rapidly from longing to sadness to hope to despair.

"We're too different, though. I'm not a socialite."

"Sweet Sara, socialites bore me to tears. I don't want anyone but you. I want to see where this can go. Where we can go. I've been trying to not rush you or draw attention to us but only because I'm feeling selfish when it comes to you. That's why, and that is the *only* reason."

A watery sound emerged from her, and she blinked rapidly. "Rhys, I don't even have a job. I'm not some boss babe like your ex. You'll be bored of *me* all too soon."

"You're wrong," he said softly. "I don't care what you do. Get a new job once the lot closes or focus on your writing. I don't care, Sara. All I care about is you."

"I have to do *some*thing. I'll go crazy if I don't."

"Then take time to choose. Just do it with me."

"But why *me*?"

"Because you are sweet and kind, talented and caring. So much so, you wear ridiculous costumes you hate because you know it makes your parents happy. You're *good*, Sara. You are comfort and quiet and...sanity. Laughter. Sweetheart, I am *not* ashamed of you. If you want to go out in public with me, let's do it. But you have to be prepared. It's hard. Quinley hated the media coverage, even though she handles things like that for a living and knows how to juggle it. It's one of the many reasons we didn't work, and—I want us to work."

He gently tangled his fingers into her hair and tugged the silky length, loving the feel of it between his fingers. "I don't want to lose you. That's why I've kept you to myself. I want *you* for Christmas, sweet Sara. And every day afterward."

Chapter Seventeen

Rhys wore her father's Santa coat, hat, and boots that evening when the lot opened but purposefully neglected to don the beard that would've disguised his handsome, well-known face. Within minutes, the image of her as his Mrs. Claus went viral.

More guards had been called in to handle the crush once word spread, but then the police came as well due to the traffic snarl of people trying to enter the lot when so few were exiting.

And even though Rhys had tried to warn her of what being seen publicly would mean, Sara wasn't prepared.

It was a lot. And she wasn't as ready as she thought she would be. But she reverted to her corporate boardroom days of handling difficult clients and tried to roll with the punches that came in the form of questions.

So many questions. When did they meet? How long had they been together? What did she bring to the table in their relationship if she was a tree-lot sales girl?

Rhys had gotten angry at that and skewered the man—a reporter—with a glare. He'd taken her hand and kissed it, holding it against his chest as he'd told the crowd they'd answered enough questions, and if they weren't buying a tree, they had to clear the lot.

The trees sold out again, with the only hold up being how fast she and Rhys could take their money and smile for photos. By the end of the evening, the lot was empty of even the smallest tree, and she and Rhys collapsed inside the red camper, still dressed as Santa and Mrs. Claus.

If she'd had any doubts about whether or not he was embarrassed of her, those had ended with his sharp shut downs to the ruder questions, and the way he'd attempted to protect her physically and verbally at every turn.

"Are you okay?"

He looked so worried, so frightened that she was going to bolt from the chaos they'd just experienced, that she got up from where she leaned against the dinette table and sat on Santa's lap, wrapping her arms around his neck. "That? *Pffft.* It wasn't that bad. And we sold all the trees, and you didn't have to buy them."

Rhys chuckled softly at her words, the tension draining from him slightly as he cuddled her closer. "I didn't have to buy them the first time. But I am glad it helped your parents."

"They'll be thrilled we sold out again," she said. "Best present ever under the circumstances."

"Good. Now I want to give you *your* Christmas present."

"Rhys, I told you I don't want gifts from you."

"Even though I know you'll really like this one?"

Curiosity got the best of her. "What is it?"

He grinned and pressed a kiss to her lips. "It's a surprise. Let's go."

"What? You mean now? Where? I need to change. *You* need to change."

He chuckled and stood with her in his arms, carrying her toward the camper door. "No. I think what we're wearing is perfect."

. . .

Less than an hour later, Sara pounced on Rhys inside the rented vehicle when she realized where Rhys had taken her on his private jet. The flight had been short but secretive, and Rhys's boyish grins and visible satisfaction had kept her guessing as to their destination.

But when she saw the hospital sign and knew he'd brought her to see her mother, she'd melted, turning and kissing him like a woman possessed.

She was still kissing him when the vehicle rolled to a stop, and she vaguely heard Axel's exit.

"Come on, sweet Sara. Time to see your gift."

She fought back tears as Rhys got out first, then held her hand as they entered the hospital and were immediately shown to her mother's private room—another gift from him she couldn't protest because it was for her mother.

But the closer they got to the doorway, the more terrified Sara became. She gripped Rhys's hand to the point of bruising, but she couldn't help it. She hadn't seen her mother since that one time right after the accident, right after she'd *died* on the table, and that visit had lasted seconds due to her mom's delicate condition.

Rhys paused outside the door to give her a moment to collect herself before they went inside.

Her mom and dad were both visibly surprised, and the smiles they wore when they saw her meant the world.

Her mom was still hooked up to tubes and oxygen and far too many things, but she was awake, if drowsy, and loved seeing Sara in her Mrs. Claus costume.

She loved seeing Rhys as Santa even more. Her mother's face lit up with pleasure, her gaze sparkling despite the visible haziness caused by the pain meds.

Sara made the introductions, cheeks rosy due to the knowing looks her parents gave her, and they settled in for a short visit.

Her father got up to speak to Rhys, giving Sara his chair by the bed. She was about to sit down when she spotted the tree on the bedside table and sucked in a breath.

The small tree held glittery, gemmed trinkets just like the raccoon Rhys had given her. There was a Santa and Mrs. Claus, a fairy, an elf, a squirrel. So many. And she knew in an instant who had sent the gift. To cheer her mother up and remind her of what waited for her once she got better.

Her heart pinched, and tears flooded Sara's eyes when she turned to see Rhys watching her.

She blinked hard and fast, not wanting to upset

her mother, but—the sweetness of the gift gutted her. Rhys was more than his money. He was kind gestures and his willingness to wear silly costumes and send meaningful gifts to people he didn't know, just because.

He was everything.

And while they were still new and had a world of what-ifs in front of them, right here, right now, she knew she was all in. No matter what the future held.

He was right. She'd been judgy in her thinking. Rhys was more than his money and net worth. Just as she was more than what people saw from the outside as an unemployed woman working for her parents.

Thank you, she mouthed softly.

Rhys winked at her, and she quickly dashed away the tears before her mom could see them.

Happy tears were good tears, and these were all good.

Thanks to Rhys, she'd found her Christmas spirit. It was right in front of her from the moment she'd met him, wearing that stupid raccoon costume.

Christmas Eve two years later...

Sara adjusted the sparkling raccoon on the tree until it hung perfectly and then took a step back to admire the eclectic collection of ornaments.

For their first Christmas together, Rhys had gifted her with her own set of trinket ornaments like the ones he'd sent to her mother at the hospital. He'd added to the collection last year, and she suspected she'd receive a few more this year.

They now decorated her favorite tree, the one in her home office that represented the many characters of her popular children's series.

After they'd flown to see her parents, they'd spent Christmas at the hospital. Afterward, she'd insisted on helping to care for her mom in her recovery, and in her free time, she wrote and illustrated to her heart's content when she wasn't in Rhys's arms.

He'd worked remotely from the tree farm a lot that year, just to stay close to her. He'd even helped out on the farm, earning Buck's grudging respect and friendship, as well as her father's.

By the time her mom was back on her feet, Rhys had discovered Sara's finished work and insisted she go the next step and publish.

So she had. And she hadn't looked back. To date she'd done book signings at stores and libraries, and she'd even embraced wearing the silly costumes to visit children's wards in hospitals to read to the sick kids. She'd loved every moment of it, even though it meant smiling for more cameras than the norm due to her relationship with Rhys and being followed by guards.

She didn't mind, though. While some might think her success was linked to Rhys, she knew her books appealed to kids who couldn't care less who she dated. Her new career as a children's author also allowed her the freedom to travel with Rhys whenever he had a meeting out of town. They explored whatever city they were in, ate the best burgers each had to offer, and fell more deeply in love.

Last Christmas, Rhys had taken her for a walk in

the snow beneath the twinkling stars over the farm and asked her to marry him. She'd said yes, of course. And they'd gotten a license and shocked the world when they'd flown a few close friends to the farm and exchanged their vows deep amid the quiet of the towering pines and snow-capped limbs.

Rhys had been busy designing as well. He'd built them a modest home on the farm to stay in when they visited, as well as a home in Carolina Cove near the river, near her parents' tree lot, so that they could stay with them whenever they were in town.

Now Sara watched her husband stare out the cottage window at the falling snow and sighed with contentment. If someone had told her how much her life would change after making that last-minute trip to Carolina Cove to cover the tree lot, she would've called them crazy.

Because now?

She bit her lip and carefully padded over to stand behind him, sliding her arms around him. "Do you see Santa?"

"I'm your Santa," he growled in that toe-curling voice. "Come sit on my lap, sweet Sara."

She laughed and squeezed him tighter. "You say that now, but you promised to keep me warm, and yet you're out here."

Their beautiful little cottage on the farm was perfectly warm enough, but she loved her husband sleeping next to her in the bed and knew the moment he'd left it. "Can't sleep?"

"I heard the guys making the delivery. Think your dad will like the new tractor?"

Rhys spoiled all of them and insisted on becoming an investor in the farm to help her parents out. He said it was a business decision on his end, a write-off, but she knew better. "I think he'll be a bit embarrassed but as excited as a kid in a candy store. He knows the farm needs it."

Rhys turned and pulled her around to face him, cuddling her close.

"And what about you? Anything particular you wanted for Christmas that you didn't tell me about?"

She smiled up at him and then used him to balance herself as she rose to her tiptoes to kiss him. "Maybe."

Rhys drew back, frowning. "What?"

She tried again, this time kissing the frown away until he bent and pulled her up against him, carrying her as he walked toward the oversized chair near the hearth.

He sat down, gently arranging her to sit facing him comfortably. "Tell me."

"I don't think *this* is how I'm supposed to sit on Santa's lap," she murmured, trying her best to keep a straight face and blink innocently.

Rhys's hands tightened on her hips in warning, though his lips quirked up at the corners. "Tell me, wife."

"Well, I was thinking we might remodel a bit."

"Remodel? You don't like the house?"

She brushed her hand through his hair at his ear, noting he'd need a trim soon. "I love our home. The house is perfect—almost. We'd just need to change the sitting room a smidge."

"Because?"

She wrinkled her nose. "We kind of forgot something? When we were going over all those designs and plans and things? Isabel has one, and now...I want one too."

"You want...an art studio? Something separate from your writing office?"

"Not quite."

"Sara...I can't read your mind. What would you like?"

She loved the feel of his cool hair against her fingertips. "You'd do that? Just give me...whatever I want?"

"You know I will. If I can, that is."

She slid her hand behind his head to his nape, staring down at the man she loved more than anything or anyone in the world. Except... "I want to change the sitting room into a nursery and playroom. Right there beside my office."

She'd never seen Rhys speechless, but she felt the moment he understood what she was saying.

"A nursery?"

"Mmm."

"So you...want to try to have a baby? Get pregnant?"

She canted her head to one side, struggling to maintain her neutral expression. "Would you mind?"

He had to clear his throat to speak, and when he did, his words were husky. "Not at all. I especially like the trying part."

She squeezed his nape a bit and leaned forward to kiss him. "I like the trying part too," she said against his lips. "I'm pretty sure that's why I'm already pregnant."

"Ahhh, sweet Sara, I was beginning to wonder if you'd ever tell me."

She drew back, frowning. "Wait, what?"

Rhys smiled up at her, looking quite satisfied that he'd surprised her.

"Do you really think I can't see the differences in your body? I know it as well as my own."

She lowered her forehead to his. "You *knew*?"

"Suspected," he said as though trying to soften the blow that her surprise wasn't a surprise after all.

"Why didn't you *say* anything?"

He kissed her softly, slowly, drawing out the kisses until she felt hazy and muddled and melty.

"Some things are worth the wait, sweetheart."

She pressed herself closer and kissed him again. "Well, we might be pregnant, but I hope we can still practice the trying part. A lot. I'm starting to realize pregnancy hormones are quite...intense."

Her laughter rang out as he abruptly stood and carried her over to the couch, carefully lowering her to the cushions.

The lights from the tree twinkled over them, and she wrapped her arms around her husband, holding him as close as she possibly could as they kissed. It wasn't everyday a girl got a loving, wonderful, gorgeous billionaire for Christmas.

And this one? He belonged to her.

I hope you've enjoyed A BILLIONAIRE FOR CHRISTMAS. **While not officially a Blackwell brother, I think Rhys's story fits in quite nicely. Keep reading for an**

excerpt from OFF-LIMITS LOVE, the next book in the Blackwell Brothers series:

"And another one bites the dust," Finn Blackwell heard his youngest brother say as they stood shoulder to shoulder and watched as Elias, Finn's twin, proposed to the woman he loved.

Hudson's hand clapped across Finn's shoulder and squeezed.

"You know you're next, right? Because I'm certainly not getting married anytime soon," his kid brother said with a wicked grin. "I'm having way too much fun for that."

Finn narrowed his gaze at Hud and shook his head. "You'll wind up with something *not* so fun if you're not careful."

Hudson's grin widened. "I'm being careful. No worries."

Hudson paused and then jerked his chin toward Finn's left. "Looks like tonight's your night. She's eyeing you hard, bro. And...now she's coming over."

"Don't," Finn bit out, knowing Hud's welcoming grin and flirty attitude had undoubtedly encouraged the woman in question to make a move.

Finn had seen her staring at him but had purposefully avoided eye contact after that initial look. Mostly because he already knew the outcome.

"You've got this. Don't be nervous," Hudson said in a low tone. "Just...do that strong, silent, broody thing you do so well. She'll love it."

"Wow, talk about romantic," the woman said as she joined them.

Finn practically vibrated with frustration when he watched Hudson flash them both an easygoing grin.

"Isn't it? Excuse me, but I've got somewhere to be. You two have fun," Hud said. "Talk to you later, Finn."

"Oh, I like your name. Finn," the woman repeated, blinking up at him, "I'm Gabby."

She held out her hand, and he reluctantly lifted his to shake, releasing it quickly to glance outside again. Quinley looked ready to cry as she nodded and said yes, and Elias placed the ring on her finger.

The crowd gathering inside the newly designed restaurant for the soft opening erupted in cheers and applause. Finn clapped along with them before turning to find the woman who'd spoken to him staring up at him, waiting for him to carry his side of their conversation.

She was strikingly beautiful. Her long blond hair curled softly around her shoulders and her dark-eyed gaze was direct and self-assured. *Expectant.* Yeah, she didn't look to be the type of woman who ever got dismissed or ignored. And while he knew he held his own because of the way bolder women approached him the rare times he left his "safe zone", they never stuck around once they heard him speak.

He inhaled a breath, feeling his pulse pick up speed when her full lips curved in an alluring smile.

"Wait a sec, are you the twin? I heard that Elias had a twin," the woman said in a sultry voice, her head turning to gaze out at the happy couple before shifting toward him once again. No doubt comparing them.

Finn opened his mouth to speak, to say that he was, when he felt his tongue and vocal cords lock up. He clamped his mouth shut to avoid the stutter that plagued him whenever he felt the slightest bit anxious or stressed, and he tried desperately to calm the anxiety that had appeared with her arrival.

Around his family he was fine. He could speak clearly and freely without issue unless angered, but to anyone else? To gorgeous women?

He grimaced at the life-wrecking flaw and then watched as the woman's expression changed when he *still* didn't speak. He tried—he really did—but then just shook his head and made a low grunt as he turned on his heel to walk away, hearing the woman's sharp gasp at his rudeness and catching the flash of disbelief that crossed her face before he ran away like a coward.

Another woman apparently joined the first because he heard them talking about him as he dodged the people gathered. He heard the woman call him a jerk and a caveman having no manners.

Finn made his way to a far corner of the penthouse restaurant, snagging a drink along the way to wait until Elias and Quinley reentered the restaurant and the soft opening officially began.

Finn downed the drink and snagged another as the happy couple reentered Haven and greeted their guests. More cheers erupted as they were surrounded with hugs and congratulatory murmurs.

He remained in the corner, tucked deep into an alcove where most couldn't see him, and took it all in.

Hudson's earlier assessment was spot on. His brothers had fallen like dominoes over the last few years. Brooks was first and early on, considering he now had three baby girls and a son to raise, but more recently Dawson, followed by Alec and Cole. Now his twin.

He stared at his brothers and realized they

looked happy. Ridiculously so as they stood with their wives and fiancées pressed to their sides. And they deserved that happiness. His older brothers especially, since they were the ones who'd given up the most to work long, hard, grueling hours to make ends meet after their parents had died in a car accident when Alec had just turned eighteen.

Maybe that was the key. They deserved to find love and settle down whereas he...didn't.

Not when it was his fault their parents had died in the first place.

Hours later, Finn rolled to a stop outside his house, feeling more than a little out of sorts after watching Elias propose to Quinley.

In the six months, Elias had been more like his old self, more the soft-hearted, laidback kid Finn remembered from before their parents' deaths. It was good to see the change after so many years watching Elias lock himself away from anything and anyone that might cause him to feel too much. To risk the pain of being left behind again.

He was happy for his twin. Jealous, too. He'd embarrassed himself horribly at the grant dinner last year and again tonight when he'd tried to converse with the beautiful woman who'd approached him.

Finn got out of his truck, the screech of its salt-corroded hinges combining with that of a woman's scream.

He thought he imagined it at first or that the sound had come from one of his farm animals, but he scanned the area in the sudden stillness and silence that followed.

The scream came again, the terror and fear in it chilling his blood.

He traced the sound to his neighbor's home and ran in that direction. Charlie was a crotchety old man who lived alone, but that scream had definitely come from the direction of Charlie's house.

The woman's scream prompted disgruntled murmurs from the miniature donkey and other animals he had yet to put away in the barn for the night, but Finn ignored them for now and vaulted over the wood fence separating their properties.

He kept going, hoping the noise of him clamoring through the brush along the fence line would scare away any snakes that might be underfoot in the pine needles.

The woman's scream came yet again, higher pitched and desperate, but he couldn't make out what she said. Possibly a name?

He spied her standing in front of Charlie's worn, small home, whirling round and round as though desperately looking for something, panic etched on her face.

He slowed to a stop in front of her, panting for air as he watched her eyes widen in alarm at his sudden appearance.

The woman's entire body trembled, and tears flooded her eyes and glittered as she stared at him. "My daughter. She's *gone*. Emi! *Emi, where are you!*"

Finn turned and listened carefully, straining to hear any rustling or cries over the sound of his heart thumping loud in his ears. Nothing. He didn't hear anything but the distant traffic from the nearby road leading to the island and sirens rapidly approaching.

Police lights flashed, and in seconds, two patrol cars arrived with a crunch of sand and gravel and dust, rolling to a stop beside the car parked beside Charlie's old truck.

Finn froze at the sight and noise, watching as uniformed officers emerged, their headlights and the flashing lights blinding him and sending his mind ricocheting back to that night so long ago. To the waning evening sky and being trapped in the car with his parents after the accident. How the police lights had hurt his eyes as they'd flashed and flashed.

He'd screamed at his parents to say something, to talk to him, staring into his mother's lifeless eyes all the while.

Finn sweated from his run and lunge over the fence, stress and panic sliding through his body as that night and this one blended together like misshapen globs of paint spilled from buckets and mixing.

"You reported a missing child?" one of the cops asked.

"Yes, my daughter, Emi. She's four."

"You the father?" the cop asked Finn.

He stared at the man, frozen in that space between past and present, as the woman spoke.

"No, he's not. I screamed for Emi, and he came running out of the woods. I don't know him," the woman said.

Four more police officers now joined them as the drive filled with vehicles and flashing lights, and Finn felt all of them staring at him like he was a pervert on the prowl. His head whirled as anxiety filled him, and his throat locked up as tight as the rest of the muscles in his body.

"You're not exactly dressed for a walk," the cop said, eyeing Finn's dress clothes and shoes. "What were you doing in the woods?"

Finn blinked at the man and opened his mouth but struggled to find the words. Frustration roared through him, upping his blood pressure. "Sh-she…" It was all he could get out, and he cursed silently.

"What's your name, buddy? You got any ID on you?"

Finn released a breath and opened his mouth again, searching the police officer's faces to find one he recognized. He knew a lot of the local force but not all of them. "F-f-f—"

"Come on, dude. We don't have time for this," the officer growled. "Do you know where her little girl is? What were you doing in the woods?"

Finn fisted his hands at his impairment and shook his head in an adamant no. The cop snorted.

"Let's see some ID. *Now*. You got any weapons on you?"

Finn shook his head again, the stress and adrenaline setting his blood and brain on fire even as it locked him up from the inside. The cop jerked a thumb to the closest patrol car.

"You hand over ID and cooperate," the cop said, "or we put you inside until we figure out why you're roaming the dark when a little girl is missing."

Finn silently cursed again, because his wallet

was in his jacket—which was still in the truck he'd abandoned when he heard the woman scream.

He lifted his hand to point toward his house, but he moved too quickly. The cops began yelling, and two pulled their weapons while the others put their hands on their guns to be ready.

Finn quickly spread his hands wide and slowly lifted the other away from his body, aware of the woman's wide-eyed gaze on him and the horror on her face as she watched one of the officers step up to cuff him. Like *he* was the reason her daughter was missing instead of a neighbor trying to help.

The cops kept asking him questions, demanding ID, but his throat wouldn't cooperate. Stupid *freaking* stammer. He'd hated his impairment his entire life, but right now, it appeared it was going to land him in jail until the mess was sorted out.

His heart pounded, anxiety riddling his body with a mixture of past and present and the nightmares that came from the police presence.

One of the cops moved close enough to empty Finn's pockets and found several dozen business cards for Haven. He'd taken them from the soft opening tonight so that he could put them up on the notice board outside the barn and to set out at the produce stand Saturday morning. To help promote Elias's new restaurant.

"He's got a bunch of these on him," one of the officers said.

"Soft opening was tonight," another said. "My wife's mom is a waitress there. Could be why he's dressed up."

"Is that why?" cop one asked.

Mortified by his weakness and beyond angry at himself, Finn nodded, vaguely wondering if the cop would call the restaurant and ask to speak to someone. Maybe Elias or one of his brothers would come to the phone and understand when the cop described the situation. Then again, the last thing he wanted was for his brothers to know about *this*.

The other cops stood grouped around the woman as she told them that she and her daughter had let Charlie's dog out to potty. The woman looked away for a second, and both were gone. Her uncle, the owner of the house, had gone to look for them.

Finn frowned, not realizing Charlie had a niece or any family. Not that it mattered.

A few of the cops left and spread out to go look for the girl while two stayed behind with him and the woman.

"You live around here, buddy?" This question came from the cop on his right.

Finn nodded again and jerked his head toward his farm. If Charlie returned, he'd be able to identify him, but Finn hadn't visited in a few weeks, and he certainly hadn't met Charlie's niece.

"That's Blackwell Farm," one of the older cops said, squinting at him as though he took a harder look at Finn. "You a Blackwell?"

He nodded again.

"Mak! I found her! I found her!"

Every head swiveled in the direction of Charlie's voice as he broke through the darkness at the edge of the house not far from where Finn had emerged.

Finn watched as the woman let out an anguished cry and ran toward Charlie and a little girl, who looked dirty and teary but otherwise okay.

Charlie turned the little girl over to his niece the moment she skidded to a stop in front of them and dropped to her knees, clutching the child tight to her chest.

"Emi, *where* have you been? I've been looking everywhere for you," the woman said.

"Maisy," the little girl cried.

The woman hugged the girl tight again, kissing

her and squeezing her like only a frantic, loving mama could.

"You scared me to death. Don't *ever* run off like that. If Maisy goes off somewhere, we find her together. Do you hear me? You don't ever, *ever* go alone."

Finn watched as the little girl's face scrunched up and she quietly sobbed, her hands curled near her chin as she stared at her mother.

The woman hugged her daughter tight once again and then rose and settled her on her hip, holding the girl while she burrowed into her mother's neck and clung like a monkey. Both were shorter than average and adorable, and across the distance, the woman met Finn's gaze, worry evident in hers as she took in the cuffs and the two cops still shadowing him.

"What's going on here?" Charlie asked, his bushy eyebrows pulling into one above his nose as he finally got a look at Finn.

"You know him?" the cop to his left asked.

"He's my neighbor. Known him for years," Charlie said.

"The kid *is* back," one of the cops said.

"You thought Finn had something to do with Emi runnin' off?" Charlie asked gruffly, surprise overcoming his expression before he shook his head with a snort. "Man wouldn't hurt a child or animal. Get those cuffs off him."

"Why didn't he say who he was?"

"Got himself a speech issue," Charlie said as he hurried closer, wheezing and out of breath, "but he's good people. Let him go."

Finn managed to unlock his jaw and took a deep breath before he said, "Heard sc-scream."

He kept his voice low, hoping Charlie's niece wouldn't hear him if nothing else. He was embarrassed enough that the cops closest to him heard.

"Why didn't you say that earlier?" the first one asked, releasing the cuffs.

Finn wanted to roll his eyes at the cop not understanding that a speech issue, as Charlie put it, might interfere with someone *speaking*, but simply shifted his arms in front of him to rub his wrists. "St-stutter w-wouldn't l-l-let."

The men seemed to finally understand and shifted uncomfortably. Like they were embarrassed for him. Stutters in kids were acceptable, even cute. But on an adult man? Not so much.

"Yeah, well, look, we didn't know what was going on," the first cop said. "I'm sure you understand why we cuffed you, given the girl was missing and the woman said you came out of the woods. You're free to go now."

"A word of advice," the second cop said. "Carry a card or something that explains your situation. It might help if anything like this happens in the future."

Finn nodded once but didn't hesitate. He didn't look at the woman, didn't look at Charlie or *any* of them as he stalked back toward the woods and home, vowing not to leave his farm again unless he absolutely had to.

Handcuffed. *That's* what he got for trying to help a screaming woman. It didn't matter that she was Charlie's niece. Or that she'd had nothing to do with the officers' responses and actions.

It simply proved to him that no matter what he did, he'd never have a normal life, and it was past time to accept it.

Get OFF-LIMITS LOVE and the rest of the Blackwell Brothers series.

THE BLACKWELL BROTHERS SERIES:

- BABY BE MINE
- SECOND CHANCE WEDDING
- THE GETAWAY GUY

- A BILLIONAIRE FOR CHRISTMAS
- OFF-LIMITS LOVE
- FLIRTING WITH FOREVER

Love Carolina Cove? I have other series set there! Check out this excerpt from SEASCAPES AND VEGAS MISTAKES, book one in my Carolina Cove Series.

CHAPTER ONE

Hey, I can tell you're exhausted from your week in Vegas but what's up with you?" Amelia asked, sliding Izzy a searching glance from the driver's seat. "I thought you'd be bouncing off the walls with excitement."

Isabel Shipley—Izzy to her friends and family—lifted a hand to rub her upper chest and wondered if it was time to break down and take something for the anxiety plaguing her ever since waking up in her hotel room this morning on her last day in Las Vegas.

The rumpled bed had said a lot of things, but it was the running shower and suddenly pounding head that wouldn't allow her to put two and two together and come up with anything other than sheer panic. Especially when a glance at the bedside clock gave her barely an hour to get to the airport and through Vegas security for her flight back home to Carolina Cove, North Carolina.

Given her frantic state to get out while the gettin' was good, she'd scrambled into clothes she'd purposely left out because she *always* ran late and grabbed the suitcase she had haphazardly packed the day before on a break from the gallery. After a last horrified glance at the open bathroom door and the scrumptiousness she left behind, she'd made a run for the hills and hopefully the return of her sanity.

She didn't *do* things like this. Ever.

So why had she?

Adrenaline had given her just enough mindfulness to hail a taxi, but the TSA line was long and she'd had to freaking *run* for her gate, arriving mere seconds before the door to the plane shut behind her as the last one to board.

Head throbbing from the stress ice pick stabbing her brain, she'd curled up against the window, her mind racing with questions and embarrassment as memories of the previous night surfaced until she fell into a fitful doze that came from too much stress, not enough sleep, a physical soreness that brought a blush to her cheeks.

Hours after leaving the hotel room and Vegas behind, her mind still hadn't come up with any logical answers. Truthfully, she couldn't even blame the champagne she'd drunk.

She'd only had three glasses over a span of time, but her excitement and adrenaline had known no bounds. And what better way to celebrate the completion of her first *real* showcase than with a tall, dark, and very gorgeous man?

He'd made her tingle. Like, seriously, *tingle*. She hadn't known such a thing was possible. Even more amazing, he'd seemed genuinely interested in her art and process, which was *such* a turn-on itself.

He also knew her cousin Michael and had attended her showcase because of it—which made him safer than the average Joe.

"Izzy? Seriously, you're worrying me. What's up?" her best friend asked.

Izzy watched as Amelia ran a hand over her rapidly expanding belly in a soothing-mama gesture and swallowed hard. She had to snap out of it. If anyone should be freaking out, it was Amelia. She was the one with twins on the way.

Izzy nodded to herself. *Suck it up, buttercup.* What was done was done. She and Everett had flirted, sipped luscious champagne, played blackjack and...made a bet. Which was how she'd wound up listening to the shower spray in the next room.

Winner gets a kiss, he'd said.

Loser has to— "I-I...I'm fine. Just really, *really* tired." Because while her challenge hadn't been anything outrageous, it *had* led to the aftermath.

"But your show was a success? You texted and said you'd scored some good commissions and would text me later to tell me details."

Thankful for the distraction, Izzy turned her attention to the passing scenery. "Yeah, sorry about that. I went to the bar for a drink and...talked to friends."

Friend, rather. That's where she'd met him again. The handsome not-so-stranger who'd wandered through the gallery around each of her paintings as though looking over a Monet or something equally amazing. Everett had introduced himself as a long-time friend of her cousin Michael's, said that he'd seen her name on the signs about the gallery show, and remembered Michael bragging about his talented artist cousin and the timing of her upcoming show.

They'd chatted briefly, her entire body humming with excitement because he was so...*so fine.*

But it wasn't until later when she'd met up with him in the bar that things had gone from casual conversation to major flirtation.

"I thought as much. You know, sometimes it really comes down to the people you know, which is why it's so important to get out there. So? Tell me. Who bought your work? Anyone famous?"

Izzy frowned. She'd stayed so busy in Las Vegas prepping for the show after the last-minute inclusion that she hadn't had time to miss home. But now that she was here?

The familiar sights and traffic signs pointing to Carolina Cove brought tears to her eyes and comfort to her soul.

Or maybe it was the relief that she could almost shut herself inside her apartment and pretend the last twelve hours hadn't happened?

Or relive them.

To be honest, it was a toss-up as to which she'd prefer.

How could a thirty-two-year-old woman get herself into such a pickle?

God forbid she ever admit this, but maybe her mother was right? She was too old for this. The games that came with dating and...

It's not dating when it's a one-night stand.

Which she didn't do.

Ever.

Except with someone Michael knows?

Her cousin wasn't a saint by any means, but she was pretty sure he wouldn't want to go to a business meeting and find out what had happened to his "kid cousin" in Vegas. And if memory served, Michael and Everett were currently working on a project.

Great. Oh, great.

"Iz?"

She had to really focus to remember Amelia's question. "Um, I-I don't know. The buyers finalized everything with the curator. I'll get more details this week, I'm sure. There...wasn't much time there at the end." Because she'd finished the show floating on a cloud, having made plans to meet Everett to celebrate the completion.

"Well, it's fantastic. I'm so proud of you," Amelia said, sliding Izzy another glance from across the way as she crossed the bridge toward Carolina Cove.

"Thanks. I mean, they could always change their mind but—"

"No buts. It's awesome and doubtful that would happen, so accept the sales as a win. I'm happy for you."

"Yeah. It's just...surreal." *In so many ways.*

She appreciated Amelia's support. Her friend was the best, softhearted and understanding and supportive even though Izzy's crazy ideas weren't always thought through.

"Okay, so, you're only minutes away from home. Take today off to recoup and rest, and then you can hit the ground running tomorrow."

"Yeah, I think I might." Sleep was good. It would bring clarity. Right? Maybe then she could figure out exactly how she'd gone from being a not-so-wild child to waking up with a virtual stranger.

She'd had boyfriends. Two long-term ones and a handful of wannabes. But despite what people—especially her mother—might believe about artists and her so-called bohemian lifestyle, she wasn't a casual hookup kind of girl.

And other than talking and laughing and kissing —a *lot*—she wasn't sure when the scales had tipped during the night. Only that she'd allowed Everett to walk her to her hotel room in the wee hours of the morning after all their fun—and then invited him inside.

"Thanks again for picking me up."

"Absolutely. The timing couldn't have worked out better. I can drop you off and head to the film location to look around and still make it home early. I want to do something special for Lincoln's birthday.

Especially since this is our last birthday alone for a while."

Izzy watched as Amelia slid her hand over her pregnant belly again and loved how happy her friend seemed to be. Pregnancy definitely agreed with her. "Good thing I have my sunglasses on," she teased. "You're absolutely glowing."

Amelia laughed, her earrings brushing her shoulders as she shrugged.

"I feel like it. I mean, it's weird but I have all of this *energy*. I'm told it's not the norm and usually the opposite is true, but I think I could climb mountains with energy to spare."

Izzy thought of how tired her older sister, Allie, had been during her pregnancies and shook her head. Definitely not the norm. "Just don't overdo it," Izzy said, wishing she could borrow some of that energy right now. Maybe then she wouldn't feel as though she'd been dragged out to sea by a riptide and been swimming against the current for days.

"Oh, I won't. I couldn't if I wanted to. Lincoln has been waiting on me hand and foot when I get home from work, and no one on set will let me lift a finger. Oh! Crap."

"What?"

"Well, before I forget...I ran into the Babes while you were gone."

"And?"

"I hate to say it, but your mom *insists* we use her house for the baby shower you're hosting. I hope that's okay? When I told them we were going to have it downstairs at London's Lattes, the Babes...well, they made it *really* hard to say no."

No doubt they had. The Babes rarely took no for an answer to anything. But why should they when the five older women had been catered to their whole lives?

During the summers of '58 and '59, four prominent Carolina Cove neighbors and friends had given birth to baby girls. One even had a set of twins. The proud mothers had taken the babes for daily strolls in their prams—and the locals had nicknamed them the Boardwalk Babes—a name used to this day by the now sixty-somethings.

All in all, Izzy had four pseudo aunts and ten "cousins," seven female and three male—with the twin Babes each having a set of twins of their own—ranging in age from mid-forties all the way down to Izzy's thirty-two. Growing up, it had sucked to always be the youngest. Even more so because not only had her two older sisters treated her like the baby but all of her "cousins" had as well. She'd always been the kid sister no one wanted tagging along to dampen their fun.

"Okay," Amelia said, turning down the street toward London's Lattes and pulling to a stop behind Izzy's VW Bug convertible. Betty the Bug might be old, but she was still just as pretty as the day Izzy had bought her. Minus a little sun damage the south was known for.

"Need help getting in?" Amelia asked.

"No. I've got it. Thanks."

Izzy had rented the apartment above the coffee shop a little over a year ago when London Cohen, owner of London's Lattes, had met and then married a northern transplant who'd moved to the beach with his adopted children. Making rent wasn't always easy with her sporadic sales, but there was no denying being on her own gave Izzy a sense of freedom and independence she'd longed for after far too many years under her parents' roof.

Living a minimalist lifestyle made it easier to live sale to sale, but it didn't leave much in the bank afterwards. Not that her parents needed to know that. But thankfully with her commissions from the Vegas showcase, she now had a cushion that would allow her to breathe for at least six months. She would put that time to good use.

Her mother had never understood why Izzy felt the need to move out of their garage apartment into an apartment several blocks away, but Izzy knew if she ever had a hope of proving her abilities and worth, she had to stand on her own. Even if it meant giving up more than a few luxuries. Life was about more than just things. It was experiences and moments...moments she captured and painted because she couldn't imagine doing anything else with her life—no matter what her family said.

"Okay, so get in there and get some rest. You don't seem like yourself, and you'll need all the energy you can muster now that the Babes are involved in the baby shower. I have a feeling things might be a little over-the-top now."

"Ain't that the truth," Izzy muttered, pulling her lips into a wry twist of dread. If her mother and the rest of the Babes knew one thing, it was how to entertain. Nothing could be simple. A party—especially a baby shower welcoming a new life into the world—would be "Babe-ified" in the extreme.

"Sorry. I know I should've protested more, but you know how they can be."

"Trust me, I know," Izzy said truthfully. "And it's

not a problem. I'm used to dealing with my mother and the Babes. No worries." While navigating the Babes might make shower prepping more stressful, Izzy wouldn't be responsible for footing the bill on the Babes' many additions to the planning. If nothing else, that was a win for her in a time when she needed to bank and save as much as she could for a rainy day.

"Iz?"

Izzy was halfway out the door when Amelia stopped her. "Yeah?"

"What's with the ring? You're pretty eclectic but that's not exactly your usual style," Amelia said with a wry expression and a little laugh.

Izzy glanced down at the gaudy, sparkling double dice ring she wore on the ring finger of her left hand. One she'd thought about taking off on the plane but hadn't because of the memories it now held in the somewhat sensual-coated space in her brain from last night.

The fun of three glasses of bubbly seemed like a good idea while she had such a great time with a handsome, charismatic man. "Oh, it's just, um, a souvenir," she said, swallowing hard because of the way her heart began to pound in her chest when an image appeared in her mind. The champagne-coated edges of her memories sharpened, and she zeroed in on the moment her gorgeous companion had slid the ring onto her finger, a smile on his seductive lips that she'd matched with one of her own.

"Good thing. For a second there I thought you'd gone and gotten married in Vegas."

Izzy released a laugh that sounded shriller than she'd intended and slid her purse to her shoulder. "You know how it goes. What happens in Vegas stays in Vegas."

Keep reading SEASCAPES AND VEGAS MISTAKES. It's available in print, audio, and ebook on my store at KayLyonsAuthor.com or online wherever books are sold.

- SEA VIEW AND SOMETHING NEW

THE BLACKWELL BROTHERS SERIES:

- BABY BE MINE
- SECOND CHANCE WEDDING
- THE GETAWAY GUY
- A BILLIONAIRE FOR CHRISTMAS
- OFF-LIMITS LOVE
- FLIRTING WITH FOREVER

MONTANA SECRETS SERIES:

- HEALING HER COWBOY
- IT HAD TO BE YOU
- HERS TO KEEP
- MILLION DOLLAR STANDOFF
- HIS CHRISTMAS WISH
- THEIR SECRET SON

TAMING THE TULANES SERIES:

- SMALL TOWN SCANDAL
- THEIR SECRET BARGAIN
- CROSSING THE LINE
- THE NANNY'S SECRET
- SOMEONE TO TRUST

THE STONE RIVER SERIES:

- WORTH THE WAIT
- NOT BY SIGHT
- MORE THAN LOVE
- LEAD ME NOT
- CHRISTMAS AT HOLLY WOOD
- THEIR CHRISTMAS MIRACLE
- SECOND CHANCES

SMALL TOWN SCANDALS SERIES:

- BRODY'S REDEMPTION
- FALLING FOR HER BOSS
- WITH THIS MAN

SECRET SANTA SERIES:

- SECRET SANTA
- SECRET SANTA II: A CHRISTMAS TO REMEMBER

About the Author

Kay Lyons always wanted to be a writer, ever since the age of seven or eight when she copied the pictures out of a Charlie Brown book and rewrote the story because she didn't like the plot. Through the years her stories have changed but one characteristic stayed true— they were all romances. Happily-ever-after guaranteed.

Published in 2005 with Harlequin Enterprises, Kay's first release was a national bestseller. Kay has also been a HOLT Medallion, Book Buyers Best and RITA Award nominee. Look for her most recent novels with Kindred Spirits Publishing.

For more information regarding her work, please visit Kay at the following:

www.kaylyonsauthor.com

@KayLyonsAuthor (Twitter)

Kay Lyons Author (Facebook)

Author_Kay_Lyons (Instagram)

Kay Lyons, Author (Pinterest)

Romance Author Kay (TikTok)

SIGN UP FOR KAY'S NEWSLETTER AND RECEIVE UPDATES ON NEW RELEASES, CONTESTS, PRE-RELEASE BOOK INFORMATION, EXCLUSIVES AND MORE!

FAQ

FAQ ABOUT CAROLINA COVE:

Is Carolina Cove a real place?

Carolina Cove is purely fictional; however, it is **loosely** based on one of my favorite places—Kure Beach and Carolina Beach, North Carolina.

The pier is real?

Yes! And it has quite a history. Be sure to check out the Kure Beach Pier Cam for a view of Kure Beach and the Atlantic.

What about the restaurants and coffee shops and places you've mentioned in the series?

London's Lattes is based on two of my favorite local coffee shops in Kure Beach and Carolina Beach. Are there more? Yes, plenty. But those two shops I know well because I've visited fairly often while writing these stories. Neither of them on their own was perfect for what I had in mind for London's, however, so I basically combined the two and ta-da! London's Lattes was born.

Why make up a city?

One of the best things about writing fiction is that when a story appears a certain way, you can write it just that way. Carolina Cove and the characters appeared to me in story form and while Kure Beach and Carolina Beach are favorite places, I had to change some things to better fit the series as well as steer far away from any real-life persons/families for obvious reasons. Doing so, that meant also changing the name of the city, etc. But, that said, you will find a slew of similarities in the fictional city and the real ones. :)

MAKE ME A MATCH SERIES:

- ROMANCE RESET
- RULES OF ENGAGEMENT
- THE MATCHMAKER'S SECRET
- PERFECTLY MISMATCHED
- BY THE BOOK

THE SEASIDE SISTERS SERIES:

- THE LAST GOODBYE
- LATTES AND LULLABYES
- MAP OF DREAMS
- WORTH THE RISK
- LOST LOVE FOUND

CAROLINA COVE SERIES:

- SEASCAPES AND VEGAS MISTAKES
- SEASHELLS AND WEDDING BELLS
- SEA GLASS AND SECOND CHANCES
- SEA BLUE AND LOVING YOU
- SEA VIEW AND SOMETHING NEW

THE BLACKWELL BROTHERS SERIES:

- BABY BE MINE
- SECOND CHANCE WEDDING
- THE GETAWAY GUY (Coming soon)
- OFF-LIMITS LOVE
- FLIRTING WITH FOREVER